About the Author:

Colin Stanley was bor
He was educat
Starting in 1970, he work
Services before moving to the ~~Midlands~~ or
Library Assistant at the University of Nottingham.
He is the author of several books and booklets on the English
writer Colin Wilson and edits the series
'Colin Wilson Studies'
'First Novel' was published in 2000.
This novel is his second.

Publisher's Note:
It is not necessary to have read
'First Novel' to enjoy this
but it would help.

For Laura,
    Nice to have met you at last!

            Colin

            PORTOBELLO ROAD
            OCT 23, 2009

By the same Author:
❋ ❋

<u>Novel</u>

First Novel (2000)

<u>Poetry</u>

Sense-less: complete nonsense poetry (2003)
with illustrations by Maggie Guillon and Yvonne Harrison

<u>Non-fiction</u>

The 'Aylesford Review', 1955–1968: an index (1984)
Colin Wilson, a Celebration: essays and recollections
(1988)
The Work of Colin Wilson: an annotated bibliography and
guide (1989)
'The Nature of Freedom' and other essays (1990)
The Work of Colin Wilson: an annotated bibliography and
guide – Supplement to 1995 (2000)

❋ ❋

Novel 2

another novel
by

Colin
Stanley

[Author of *First Novel*]

Paufict

Published by :
Paufict
37 Quayside Close,
Trent Bridge,
Nottingham NG2 3BP
United Kingdom.

I.S.B.N. 0-946650-88-8 (Paperback)

Author's Note

❀

This is a work of fiction.
Any reference to actual events,
to real persons, living or dead,
or to real locales are intended to give
the novel a sense of authenticity.
Other names, characters, places, incidents
are purely the product of the author's imagination
or are used fictitiously.
Their resemblance, if any, to real-life
is purely coincidental

For our complete catalogue of books, write to the above address or
e-mail us at:

stan2727uk@aol.com

Visit our website at:
http://www.pauperspress.com

Part One

'...of all ordinary human experiences only sex sensations approach those which we may call "mystical"... there is a certain autumnal taste in them, the taste of something that must pass, must die, must cede its place to something else. This "something else" is the *new consciousness*...'

P. D. Ouspensky: *A New Model of the Universe*.

1

Christopher Purbright, a minor but published novelist, awoke and reached for the pen and paper which he knew to be on his bedside table. Dreams formed an important part of his fiction and he was careful to record them promptly before they escaped back into the recesses of his mind. Just a few words were necessary to stimulate the memory. These were scrawled across the paper without even opening his eyes.

Outside, the dawn chorus was gathering momentum. Spring was just around the corner. But none of this registered in Christopher Purbright's brain—having recorded the essence of his dream, he was already asleep again...

2

The rush-hour traffic on Radcliffe Road disturbed his sleep. The Lady Bay area of Nottingham was a leafy suburban haven, tucked into a vee between an arterial road and the River Trent. It was a quiet and orderly community disturbed only when Nottingham Forest played at home or when there was a Test Match at Trent Bridge. Both grounds stood nearby with fast-food outlets, pubs and small hotels spreading in all directions.

Christopher's house was a 1930's semi-detached, recently double-glazed. He had grown into the habit of sleeping with the window open even in mid-winter as he invariably awoke with a headache if starved of fresh air in the night. Consequently, he always ran the risk of being disturbed by outside noises...

His tabby cat, Brocard, was waiting impatiently in the kitchen. Scattered over the floor were the remains of a blackbird—a wing here, some feathers there, a severed head poking out from under the cooker.

"Oh no..."

The cat pushed around his legs, purring loudly in anticipation of a bumper breakfast. After all, it wasn't every morning he provided his master with such a prize. But no...instead of praise he got verbal abuse and was forced to wait what seemed like an age locked in the sitting room, looking through the glass-panelled door, as the debris was cleared.

The grisly work done, Christopher sat at the kitchen table and glared at the cat through the door.

"What a start to the day!"

He filled the kettle, took a bowl from the rack and tipped some cornflakes into it. Onto this he dropped a handful of raisins before pouring the cold milk. Meanwhile, Brocard scratched at the door and mewed insistently.

"You can bloody well wait!"

But hunger had turned him into a desperate animal and, stretching his full length, he laid his front paws on the horizontal handle of the door—the spring of which was broken—pushed forward and was in. The irresistible smell of dead bird led him on a circuitous false trail around the kitchen before, inevitably, ending up in front of the food cupboard. If he was to eat his own breakfast in peace, Christopher knew there was no alternative than to feed him straight away.

The kettle boiled. With the cat now under his feet, he stumbled to the worktop, spooned some coffee into a cup and poured on the hot water. Then, bending down, he opened the cupboard, chose a sachet of cat food and squeezed it into a bowl, grimacing as he smelt the contents.

Looking up, the calendar on the wall caught his attention with *Agent 12.30* and *Sarah* scrawled alongside today's date. These were his two appointments for the day. The thought of lunch with his agent, who would want to talk about the novel he should have been writing but in truth hadn't even started, depressed him. He would lie,

9

unconvincingly, all the time thinking of how soon he could get away to Sarah—a young student he had met late one night at the *Irish* nightclub and immediately impressed with his knowledge of Kafka. Unable to converse satisfactorily in the noisy bar, they had retired to her room in Lenton where they had spent the night and most of the following day. Kafka, as far as he could recall, had hardly been mentioned except when he had tripped over a paperback edition of *The Trial* on his way to the bathroom. That was more than a month ago and since then, every Friday afternoon, after her morning lecture, they met at her flat which she shared with another student.

3

✿ ✿

Leaving his house in Melbourne Road, he locked the door, stepped through the gap where the front gate once stood and, turning right, headed in the direction of Trent Boulevard. A fresh breeze blew into his face causing him to hunch his shoulders and turn up the collar of his jacket. He crossed the road without looking, trusting his ears, then continued until he came to the junction with the Boulevard. As he turned left he glanced right and saw the green double-decker bus approaching. But there was no panic—the tree-lined Boulevard was very long and straight and the bus still two stops away. He merely quickened his pace slightly in order to arrive at the stop just before the bus. There were five or six people already waiting outside the newsagents. No need to run.

He arrived at the stop in time to turn and wave to Alan, the newsagent, standing behind his counter, staring out into the world. Boarding the bus, he flashed his Easy Rider card at the driver and ascended the steps to the upper deck where he sat on the left so he could look into the cricket ground on his way down Radcliffe Road. This he always did, winter or summer—the mere sight of the open green field causing him to breathe deeply, relax and think of long leisurely hot days spent watching cricket. As the bus crossed the Trent Bridge, and the morning sun glinted off the slow moving water of the river, he reflected on how therapeutic and philosophical the game of cricket was. Like a good movie it unfolded slowly, sucking you in, at turns exciting and absorbing with the possibility of providing a nail-biting climax.

His thoughts were interrupted as the bus approached Nottingham Midland Station. He was to meet his agent at *Via Fossa*—a new pub created from an old and vast warehouse which backed onto the canal that ran through the city. A few years ago this was a no-go area—run-down, deserted, derelict, depressing; the shadow of Nottingham's industrial past. But now a magnificent new Magistrate's Court fronted the canal on one side with an iron footbridge linking it to the clubs, bars and re-located local newspaper offices on the other. His footsteps sounded hollow and metallic as he crossed. Turning right, he weaved his way through an assortment of wooden benches—popular on warmer nights—and into *Via Fossa* through a huge side door, obviously the original entrance to the warehouse.

Inside, the music was a little loud for his taste but he considered that this was not altogether a bad thing. He would be able to buy time by pretending not to hear his inquisitor and have a valid excuse for being economical with his words. As he ascended a flight of wooden stairs set against the far wall, he could see Lenny, his agent, already seated at one of the tables next to the glass doors that, on a warmer day, would have opened onto the balcony that overlooked the canal and the Magistrate's Court.

4

❁ ❁

Agent Lenny was in his thirties but almost completely bald. He chose to accentuate rather than hide this by having the sides and back of his head shorn close to the scalp. A pair of wire-rimmed dark glasses with small round lenses gave him a sinister appearance offset slightly by the sharp grey three-piece suit. Very much the businessman who meant business.

"Christopher!" the accent was faintly New York American tempered by ten years in the UK, "what'll you have?"

"A glass of dry white wine, I think, Lenny. How are you?"

"Hell, let's have a bottle! We'll eat—it's lunchtime. I'm very well, thank-you."

He crossed to the bar, ordered the drinks and returned with a menu.

"I'm starving," he peered at his guest over the top of his glasses, "hmmm...I'll have the lamb, I think...and you? It's on expenses."

"The lamb's always good here...I'll go for it...with a side portion of fries."

The wine arrived and Lenny ordered the food. Lifting the bottle, he examined the label:

"Chilean Sauvignon Blanc, hmmm..."

He poured two glasses and took a draught.

"Not bad... not at all bad..."

Christopher sipped tentatively from his glass. Crisp, dry, fruity, nicely chilled—it had the immediate effect of lifting his spirits and making him feel hungry.

"Well... I was with old man Crape on Monday and that gorgeous blonde assistant of his...Helen Double-Barreled-Something. He's very worried about you. Wants to see some evidence that you're honouring your contract."

Christopher's mouth went dry and he no longer felt hungry.

"Yeah...yeah," he spluttered, trying to sound matter-of-fact, "it's all in hand. I've got it all planned out—that's the most difficult part, you know—all I've got to do now is write it."

"Okay...great...so how soon can we hope to see some results?"

"Six months..."

"Six months!" Lenny almost lost his cool, recovered himself, glanced around the room where one or two people were staring in his direction, moved his face closer to Christopher and whispered forcefully:

"Listen! You are already a year behind schedule and now you say another six bloody months!"

"Lenny, Lenny...be reasonable. I'm an artist. I'm not one of your three novels a year formula writers. I can't be expected to produce works of art to a timetable..."

"Then why the bloody hell did you sign a contract to that effect?"

"Well, you know how it is. I thought I could do it but I've got a bit stuck. It'll be alright..."

"Okay...okay," Lenny held up his hands, palms outward, "so what's it called?"

14

Christopher looked apprehensive.

"It must have a title...surely?"

"Ah...yeah...uh...*Second Novel* or maybe...um...*Novel 2* ...I haven't decided."

Lenny brightened:

"Okay...that's fine...that's good. Your first novel was called *First Novel*, your second *Novel 2*. I like it... continuity, that's what the punters want. Excellent! So what's it about?"

"Well..." Christopher was seriously bluffing now, "it's going to be exactly the same story but from a different angle."

Lenny's brow furrowed menacingly:

"The *same* story!"

The emphasis on *same* made it clear Lenny was not impressed.

"Christopher...you have your readers to consider. Are they really going to go for the *same* story again when many of them were upset about how enigmatic the first was? I mean...don't get me wrong...I thought it was good, I thought it was great—I wouldn't have taken it on if I hadn't—but its attracted some very extreme reviews. That guy who quoted Christopher whatsisname at you... (Christopher Donald, was it?)..."

"Derrick..."

"Yeah, whoever; 'the novel you must not write: the novel that devotes all its energies to playing with the novel convention...' or some such crap. I'm not saying I agree with him, I mean some sad bastards can't even blow their noses without first buying a "How to..." book on the subject—which kind-of misses the point when it comes to art—but there are people out there who actually agreed with him. And now you tell me you intend to serve up the same fare again. Is this really wise Christopher? Think about it—aren't you going to be stretching it just a little bit?"

"Hmm...no, I don't think so, Lenny...um...ah, here comes the food!"
Glad of the diversion, Christopher headed for the toilets where he stood, leaning on the sink, staring at himself in the mirror:

"Think, Christopher...think!"

"And here's another thing...you use the three dots too much...much too much...you wanna cut down."

He's not letting up, thought Christopher, as he resumed his seat.

"The three dots, Lenny...good for pauses...and changes in direction...goodness me is that the time!" he feigned a glance at his watch. But Lenny was not amused.

"Céline used them a lot Lenny...to good effect...in *North*, for instance. If it's good enough for Céline..."

"Yeah, but you're *not* Céline, Christopher. Write a *Journey to the End of the Dark* and I may...just may...take you more seriously. No, it's sloppy, Chris...sloppy."

"That's bullshit, Lenny, bullshit...and it's *Night* not *Dark*...*Journey to the End of the Night*."

"Whatever," he shrugged it off, "just think about it, Chris...think about it. Now...Edinburgh Festival...this year...August. Wanna do it? They want you to read in a little tent in Charlotte Square."

"Oh!" taken by surprise, "yeah, I'll get Sarah to drive

16

me up. It's during her summer holidays..."

"Oh, they'll pay rail fare, overnight accommodation etc. ...no problem."

"Yeah, okay...send me the details."

"Will do," he took a mouthful of the lamb, served on a bed of spicy rice, "hmmm...good...try it. You're not eating."

"Well...if you'd shut up for a bit...I might get a chance!"

They ate in silence for a few minutes, Lenny greedily, not really chewing adequately and swallowing hard. There was clearly something on his mind and, to Christopher's dismay, he meant to talk about it at the earliest possible opportunity.

Christopher needed to buy time whilst his mind worked feverishly on a plot for *Novel 2*.

"Well?" Lenny was dabbing his mouth with a paper napkin.

"Sorry? The music is so loud in here," still buying time.

"For Christ's sake Christopher! I need to know how things are progressing. So give..."

"Well...shall we have some more wine? I'll get another bottle. Same again?"

"Yeah...yeah...whatever..."

He returned from the bar with the bottle and topped-up the glasses, already quite light-headed, having drunk most of the first.

"Okay...well you know how the hero of *First Novel* was himself writing a novel?"

"Yeah...yeah," impatiently.

"Well this novel is about his hero and the story is the same but from *his* perspective..."

17

Lenny's brow was rucking again:

"Christopher...do not fuck with me!"

"Lenny...I wouldn't fuck with you. You're just not my type!"

"Shut-up...how much of this have you actually committed to paper...or disc...or whatever?"

"Hah! It's all in here, Lenny," he tapped his forehead.

"And will take another six months to come out!" Lenny was not impressed.

"That's about the size of it. Have some more wine."
Lenny, in no mood for more wine, waved his arm dismissively, upsetting his glass and its contents onto the table. Before the thin line of wine could reach the edge and spill over, he slammed the paper napkin over it. This served to increase his annoyance.

"Christopher...get your ass into gear...get a grip...get it written! And have some respect for your readers..."

"Yeah...yeah..." the wine had somehow put Christopher in the ascendancy, "look, do I have to drink this myself? I'm pretty damn drunk as it is!"
Lenny sighed:

"I've had enough, thanks," he stood up, walked over to the bar and paid the bill.

"Chris...I'm off now...but remember what I said..." he started down the stairs:

"Oh...and don't forget...the three dots..."

"Dot, dot, dot...fuck off Lenny," he said, under his breath...

5

❀ ❀

Outside: a taxi cruised past. Christopher waved his arm franticly. In some Hollywood movie there would have been a squeal of brakes at this point and our hero would already be on his way to his chosen destination. But this is Nottingham, an East Midlands city in England…

There was a squeal of brakes. Christopher dived into the back of the cab and was immediately on his way to Sarah's flat in Lenton—above a Chinese takeaway. The entrance was at the back along a rubbish-strewn alleyway, up a zig-zag flight of metal steps. The door ahead was closed but, when he turned the handle and pushed, opened inwards to the kitchen. Ahead was a flight of stairs which led to the bedrooms. He called her name.

"I'm in the bedroom," came the muffled reply. He felt a tightness in his stomach upon hearing her voice. She was waiting to have sex with him; had probably been masturbating, sitting in bed, warm, ready. He called in at the bathroom at the top of the stairs. A pair of white knickers had been abandoned on the floor along with some tights. He locked the door, urinated, spread some toothpaste around his teeth with a forefinger then rinsed with water. Before unlocking the door, almost without thinking, he slipped the knickers into his pocket, and crossed the landing to Sarah's bedroom. As he had suspected, she was already sitting in bed—a large double mattress which covered two-thirds of the floor space—her back supported by pillows propped against the wall. Her long black hair cascaded over her shoulders and chest merging with the black bra which she always wore when he visited. This was part of their game…the black bra covering those huge breasts which he was not allowed to see or touch until she was ready. The game began…he undressed. She watched, and when he was down to his underpants, beckoned. As he knelt on the mattress she peeled the underpants down over his erection, looked up into his face and sucked his penis into her mouth. Placing his hands on her head he rocked gently forward and back. A picture of some Hollywood star stared back at him from the wall. The face was familiar but he could never fit a name to it. Film actors and actresses were not his forté and he could never understand why she was so obsessed with them when it was the director that was important. And Hollywood, as he had often argued with her, was just a factory which mass-produced formula movies for the entertainment of the popcorn-eating public. All the great works of art were made on this side of the Atlantic or in Asia. But…

Her tongue flicked over the end of his penis as he withdrew it, engorged and glistening, from her mouth and collapsed on the bed beside her. She immediately threw a leg over him and lowered herself onto his erection.

"Ahhhh…," they exhaled together, her flushed face coming down towards him, hair blocking out the light, salty tongue darting into his mouth. The bra pressed heavily into his flesh.

"Ohhh…"

He broke free, gasping for air. She straightened up and started to move her hips. On top of the bookcase, behind the door, a photo of her father, sister and brother in a plastic frame. No mother. She had left home, apparently, when Sarah was five.

"Oh God…"

His trousers lay in a heap on the floor, the pair of knickers drooping conspicuously (so it seemed to him) from one pocket. Encircling her waist with his arms, he pulled himself up towards her and, tipping her sideways, freed his legs, withdrew, grabbed her by the ankles and pulled her near the edge of the mattress. Kneeling on the floor between her open legs he lowered his head to her groin, lapping with his tongue. At the same time, his left hand groped across the floor to his trousers with the intention of thrusting the knickers deep into the pocket. But just as his fingers closed around the garment, Sarah grabbed his head with both hands, jerked, writhed, screamed then pushed him roughly away from her as she tried to regain her breath. In the melee, as Christopher fell backwards, the knickers looped through the air and flopped onto her breasts.

"What the…where did these come from?"

Thinking quickly:

"I…ah…found them downstairs…on the bathroom floor… must be yours…"

"No, *not* mine!" aggressively.

"Sorry…*thought* they were yours…"

"They're Lisa's. Like them?"

She held them up.

"Sorry…"

"Dirty bastard!"

Pushing him roughly onto his back, she threw a leg over and straddled him just above his knees. Christopher knew what was coming next. His penis strained upwards as she slowly reached behind her back and unclipped the bra. Covering as much of her breasts as possible with her left arm she removed it completely, throwing it at him. Reaching over to a bedside cabinet she extracted a bottle of baby oil, squirted some over her breasts and rubbed it in until the flesh glistened, tweaking her nipples with thumb and forefinger until they became erect. Backing off towards his feet, she bent and allowed the slippery skin to rub across his chest, abdomen, penis, testicles, then up again.

His breathing became sporadic, his heart beat furiously and his throat went dry.

"Oh God, Sarah...do it...do it!"

He tried to push her back down but she resisted.

Producing Lisa's knickers, she held them out to him:

"Not before you sniff these, you dirty bastard!"

"Sarah!...for God's sake!"

"Do it!"

He sniffed tentatively.

"Hold them there…breathe it in…"

"Sarah!"

"Do it!"

He acquiesced, reluctantly at first, but finding it more and more erotic, entered into the spirit of the game.

"There's a good boy. Does she smell good?"

"Yes," he conceded.

"She was screwing her boyfriend last night. I heard them through the wall. Can you smell him too?"

"Oh God!" he threw them away.

"Naughty, naughty," reaching over, breasts dangling, she retrieved them and pushed them into his face again.

"Would *you* like to fuck her?"

22

"I…yes…"

"Say, 'Yes, I'd like to fuck your friend Lisa'."

"Yes."

"And the rest."

"Yes…I'd like to fuck your friend Lisa."

"How do you know, you've never met her," she teased.

"Oh God…please Sarah, please…finish me off…or I'll do it myself."

Ignoring him:

"She's got red hair—you like that, don't you? And she's a *natural* red-head too! Can you imagine that rubbing against this gusset?"

"Oh God…"

She ran her breasts slowly down his body again, enjoying the absolute power she had over him, milking it for all she was worth. Closing her hands around her breasts, pushing them inwards, she trapped his erection in her cleavage. He came immediately, sperm shooting over her breasts and neck, dripping down onto his stomach. He breathed a long hard sigh.

"Jesus…I needed that…"

"Hmm…," she was licking the sperm from around his navel. He watched it glistening on her tongue as she waggled it from side to side, moved up his body and worked it into his mouth. He sucked on the saltiness and swallowed.

"Nice? You can let go of Lisa's knickers now. Put them in your pocket. Take them home. She won't miss them."

Her breasts brushed over his face depositing a mixture of sperm and baby oil. Her pubic hair scraped over his lips and nose as she straddled him, his tongue worked its way into the softness. She was kneeling with her shins across his shoulders, knees holding his head in place, arms and body flat against the poster of Marlon Brando on a motorcycle which covered the wall above her bed. His tongue snaked between the folds of her flesh, the juice running along his lips and dripping off his chin. Wetting his forefinger he slid it between her buttocks, pushing it deep into her anus. She squirmed and moved rhythmically as his tongue flicked around her clitoris. Losing control, her fingernails scratched at the poster bringing it down off the wall. Behind: a huge house spider, startled, scuttled away.

"Ah!…Ah!…Ah!…spiderrrr! Chris…"

Twisting her body, she jerked her knee into the side of his head, inadvertently smacking him in the eye with her fist and dislocating the finger lodged inside her.

"Ah!…ah!…my finger…oh my God, it's broken…fuck …no…no…"

End of game.

Valium

…ah…

…oh…

…a dark corridor; faint illumination from above; two doorways…one, on the left, locked…the other, on the right, no handle but moves outwards when pushed; bright sunlight streams in…he awakes…

7

❀ ❀

"Just sit down there, Chris, and I'll make you some coffee …oh…and I'll get some ice for the finger. Doc said it would help with the swelling."

Sarah left the room for the kitchen. The front door slammed, footsteps and voices were heard.

Lisa appeared at the door, her curly red hair tied into a bunch.

"Oh!" surprised, "you must be Christopher. I'm…a… Lisa."

"Hello," he could hardly look her in the eye.

"Are you alright?" she noticed the pained expression on his face.

"I…um…dislocated a finger…we've just come back from Queen's Med."

He held up his hand gingerly. Index and middle fingers were taped together.

"Oh my God! How did you do that?" the accent was, he thought, bogus upper-class, more pronounced when exclamatory...like she was making a conscious effort to suppress her roots.

"Oh…it's…you'd better ask Sarah."

"I will…" she backed out of the room.

Christopher sank back into his seat, the valium that had knocked him out before manipulation, still relaxing him.

The sound of crockery being washed came to him…and voices whispering. A loud guffaw from Lisa:

"What! And that's how he did it!"

"Shhhhh…"
Stifled giggling.
A mug smashed on the floor:
"Shit!"

8
✿ ✿

He decided in the car on the way home. Sarah listened:

"I'm going to Devon for a bit...to the flat...in Tapshed."

"Oh?" questioningly, "can I come and visit? Or drive you down?"

She already knew the answer:

"No, I'll take the train."

"Will you be away long?"

"Don't know...there's a few things I have to work out..."

"Tapshed?" her brow furrowed, straining to remember, "that's been in the news today. While I was waiting for you...at the hospital. Some little girl's gone missing or something."

"Yeah?"

"Yeah...didn't catch any details. You know how noisy it is in those accident and emergency waiting rooms. But they showed it on a map...just below Exeter."

"That's right. Look, Sarah..." the car pulled up outside of his house, "Lenny, my agent, you know, he's fixed up a reading for me at the Edinburgh Festival this year. Come if you want...you could drive me."

She brightened:

"When?"

"August...early August."

"Right...yeah...okay," she smiled.

He leaned over and kissed her primly on the cheek. Holding his injured finger aloft he stepped out of the car.

"Chris...what about Brocard?"

"Oh...next door will look after him. Thanks, anyway."

9

❀ ❀

He had made up his mind: Derby station was the most depressing place on earth…an opinion formed over many years of standing, waiting, observing.

Nearly an hour to kill before his train was due. A chill wind blew along the platform as he picked up his weekend bag and ducked into the cavernous waiting area to check the arrivals/departures screens. His train was not even listed. *W.H. Smith* glistened and beckoned like an enchanted cave. Mesmerised, he entered but didn't stay long. The bookshelves were stacked with novels by big-name authors milking their already established readership and celebrities cashing-in on their popularity or notoriety. Proof that the public wanted what the public got. He bought some mints to take the bad taste out of his mouth and left as quickly as he had come.

The Plymouth train was listed…platform 3. He mounted the steps to the covered footbridge, crossed the lines, descended onto the platform where the wind hit him again, forcing him to seek out the waiting room.

Already a small collection of would-be travellers were scattered around the seats reading magazines, paperback books or trying to entertain bored children. All *killing* time…hoping to lose their sense of the here-and-now… a sure way of making the train arrive quicker…then, on the train, more time to be *killed* until destinations were reached. That's the way our lives slip away from us, he thought, when we're not *conscious*…just killing time.

An eccentrically dressed but attractive woman came in and sat opposite him. She wore a long white figure-hugging dress, dark glasses, a red scarf on her head and a gold necklace that looked like a spider's web. Her brown hair hung in a plait which reached as far as her waist. The strap and lace black shoes raised her a good three inches from the ground and revealed black polished toenails.

He fell to thinking about how she lived her life. Original, unconventional, fun to be with, probably... inventive in bed? His finger ached...he would need to take more of the pain killers, given to him at the hospital.

At length the train pulled in. Jumping to his feet, he flung the strap of the weekend bag over his shoulder. She smiled as he opened the door and let her through. It was then that he realised she had no luggage and was probably just there to meet someone. Feeling disappointed—he had fantasised about falling into conversation with her on the train—he boarded and found himself a seat next to the window. She stood, looking up and down the platform and was still standing there when the train pulled away. He felt like jumping out, grasping her hand and pulling her on board. But he would, of course, in all probability, never see her again. The thought depressed him...all those millions of people out there who he would never get to know. He felt somehow helpless...almost devastated but then, as a beam of sunlight shone into the carriage, lifting his spirits, he felt...powerful: he *chose* not to know them.

The re-awakening English countryside flashed past his window broken by urban industrialised landscapes—Burton-upon-Trent, Tamworth, Birmingham. At the buffet car he bought a bottle of water and washed down the pills. Regaining his seat, back to the engine, he stared out at the receding view. He was never able to sleep when travelling…always too interested in what was going on inside and outside…but today…

10

…Exeter cathedral…a perfect place to levitate. Kicking His feet into the air He floats up with ease…with confidence…with control…with joy. He thinks:

'Anything is possible for me.'

Landing gracefully on his feet, He decides to walk through a stone column…one of the many supporting the vast vaulted roof.

Closing His eyes He walks towards it, feeling the coldness of it against His nose and chest. Opening them, He finds Himself on the other side of the pillar but still feels the coldness against the front of His body. Turning around, He sees that it has been left behind…on the other side…

11

He awoke just outside of Exeter having been asleep, to his astonishment, for some time. The cars on the Honiton bypass were losing their race with the train.

Another levitation dream. They were coming to him rapidly now…these dreams. Always kicking himself into the air, arching his back to gain height, pushing himself upwards. Sometimes there were people below looking up admiringly. But always that overwhelming sense of possibility and benevolent power…as if to say,

"This is nothing extraordinary. You can do it too. Use the power of your mind."

This was the first time, however, he had actually passed through solid objects. The lucidity of the dream left his senses sharpened.

Extracting a notebook from his bag, he made a few notes then concentrated on the scenery rushing past the window. There was no blurring…images were sharp and clean. He saw the complete picture not just the random pieces of a new jigsaw. Aware of his body rushing through space…aware of the blood coursing through his veins. In that moment he knew he was *part* of the picture…not separate. Part of the whole. A man with a mission…to complete…to bring together…to start from the end and finish at the beginning…

12

The beginning *was* Exeter, more accurately Tapshed, just to the south, where he was born. Everything would come together there.

As he opened the door and alighted onto the platform at Exeter St Davids, these thoughts flew away from him as if they had been physically restrained by the claustrophobic railway carriage. A small crowd gathered around him, eager to board the train and grab the best seats. They stood aside reluctantly as he pushed his way through, holding his injured hand against his chest.

The connecting train to Exmouth, calling at Tapshed, was already waiting on platform 1. Realising there was little time, he bounded up the steps of the footbridge that straddled the lines. Descending, he cracked his shin against the suitcase of an early holidaymaker laden with luggage. Swearing under his breath, he boarded the train, slumped into a seat and rubbed his leg vigorously to deaden the pain.

The doors closed and the slow climb to Exeter Central began.

13

❈ ❈

Someone…some amateur topiarist…had carved the name TAPSHED in the hedge. He remembered vaguely that it was the father of a school friend who had worked at the station prior to Dr Beeching. The signal-box had long-since been converted into a trendy shop selling picture frames…the gates which blocked the road allowing the train through, were operated remotely…watched over by video cameras. Leaving the station, he instinctively turned in the direction of Mamouth Avenue but checked himself. His parents were long since dead and the house where he was born, and where his mother was born, sold. With some of the proceeds…not wishing to break his links with the town…he had bought a small flat on the water-front…in a large courtyard complex…once a cider factory.

After waiting for the gates to lift, he walked down Station Road to the town centre. A glass of wine was what he craved as he tried to remember if there was any in the fridge at his flat. Unsure, he bought two bottles of Pinot Grigio from the off-licence at the bottom of the street, and a local newspaper from the shop next door, before heading off into the town centre. There had been a time when he had regretted all the changes that had re-shaped his home town over the last thirty years. Not drastic reconstruction …all the houses had conservation orders on them…but cosmetic…reflecting a new affluence and turning Tapshed into little more than a dormitory town for Exeter, four miles away. The main street was no longer the self-contained shopping centre consisting of small family businesses. It had become a ribbon of estate agents, antique shops, fake antique shops, wine bars, eating houses, specialist retail outlets. But somehow that didn't bother him anymore. He just rejoiced in the fact that he was one of the few true locals who still remained even if his flat was little more than a country retreat...somewhere that stirred his imagination and enabled him to work in peace.

Passing the church, he turned right through the churchyard to the high wall overlooking the estuary—one of the most celebrated views in the West Country. To the South, the river Exe spread itself wide, joining the Clyst just below Tapshed, with Exmouth visible in the distance on its eastern bank and the village of Starcross on the western side. Panning northward across the marshland, bird sanctuary and canal, Haldon Hills rose green and healthy on this early spring day. Beyond that lay the vague outlines of the eastern fringe of Dartmoor.

Clutching the railings at the top of the precipitous steps leading down to the road that ran along the river's edge...feeling its coldness...he breathed deeply, filling his lungs with air fresh from the moors. To his left he could see the converted warehouse that was Harry's studio. Harry...a friend from way-back...Yorkshireman, now settled in Tapshed...a talented photographer.

Maybe, he thought, I'll pay him a visit. He may have a bottle of chilled white in his fridge.

Ollershaw
❀ ❀

It was some time before Harry, a chubby, bald-headed man in his mid-fifties, answered the door:

"Chris! My God…this is unexpected!"

The Yorkshire accent was unmistakable despite ten years' exile in Devon.

"Yeah, I …um…needed some time to myself."

"Well, come in…I'll fix you a drink."

"Thanks. I could murder a glass of wine. I've got some here but it's not chilled."

"Um…well I haven't any in…um…you can make yourself a cup of tea, if you like."

Christopher pulled a face:

"Tea…can't stand the stuff!"

"Oh…well…coffee then…over there in the kitchen. I'm downstairs working in the studio. Make three cups and bring them down. I'll introduce you to Alison," he winked and started to disappear down the spiral staircase at the end of the room:

"What happened to your hand?"

"Oh…I'll tell you about it sometime."

The view from the kitchen area was as grand as that from the top of the churchyard steps. As he ran the water from the tap into the kettle he looked out over the rooftops of some houses that actually protruded into the river itself, to the M5 road bridge beyond with its miniature cars—just visible as they sped across. The tide was out revealing acres of unsightly mudflats. The causeway—almost immediately below, opposite the foot of the churchyard steps—extended nearly half way across the river, which was little more than a murky brown strip flowing slowly toward the sea.

Setting three mugs on a tray he spooned instant coffee into each and poured on the boiling water. Opening the fridge he found nothing but half a tomato covered in mould and, to his annoyance, an unopened bottle of Sauvignon Blanc. It looked good quality stuff so he hastily swapped it for one of the bottles he had bought.

"Harry...do you have any milk?"

"In the fridge...if there's any," a muffled reply from downstairs.

"None there, I'm afraid."

"Oh...well...we'll have it black. Is that alright love?" (a woman's voice answered in the affirmative), "yes, fine...bring it down."

So he picked up the tray and, as he was walking through the lounge, heard:

"Don't mind if my friend Christopher sits in on this, do you love? He's on the editorial board of *Fiesta*, you know. Could pull a couple of strings..."

"No, no...that's okay...really," she laughed nervously.

"Chris, this is Alison...Alison, Christopher."

Setting the tray on a small table at the bottom of the staircase, he shook hands with an attractive but, he thought, slightly overweight, young girl—about twenty years old—with shoulder-length curly blonde hair and wearing oval-shaped metal-rimmed glasses.

"Alison is a student...in Exeter. We're just doing some test shots today and we'll see where we go from there. What do you think Chris? *Fiesta* material?"

"Um...well...yes...possibly...possibly."

Christopher could feel the perspiration on his brow. He was not making a good fist of this. Looking around to hide his discomfiture:

"Nice set-up you have here Harry."

The room was littered with all the paraphernalia of the professional photographer. It was obvious Harry took his work seriously and probably gleaned a lucrative living from it.

"Right love, this coffee's a bit hot so perhaps we can make a start. A few poses with your clothes on."

The far end of the room was brightly lit by a lamp on an extending stand and boom—there being no natural light, all the windows having been boarded up. A large expanse of white material flowed down from the ceiling and sprawled over the floor upon which Alison, in a short black dress, black tights and shoes, stood awkwardly, looking anything but sexy, between two white reflector screens.

"Right now…just relax love."

Her shoulders slumped forward.

"No, no, that's *too* relaxed, love. Um…look...take your glasses off...put your hands on either side of your head…scoop your hair back…push your chest out… Great!…great! Just hold that! Brilliant!"

He moved swiftly to a camera mounted on a tripod, peered through the viewfinder, moved the entire apparatus closer to the subject and began shooting.

"Okay…take a break. That coffee should be alright now."

She moved toward them, bent over and picked up the coffee:

"Gosh…its hot under those lamps."

"You bet. You looked very good though. Now…what are you wearing under that dress?"

"Um…," she sounded breathless suddenly, as if surprised at being asked, "tights, knickers, bra…all black."

"Ah…yeah…oh dear; forgot to tell you last night. Best not to wear anything that will leave a mark on your skin—looks a bit odd, you see."

"Oh…of course…silly of me."

"No, don't worry…my fault. These are only test shots so it doesn't matter that much. But if we decide to call you back for the real thing…remember…no undies."

"Yah…okay."

"Right…can you just slip off the tights then put your shoes back on."

Christopher started to feel embarrassed:

"Harry…perhaps I ought to wait upstairs…"

"No…no…how are you going to judge," he winked, "you don't mind, love, do you?"

"No…no…not at all."

She had turned away from them, hitched up her dress, pulled the tights down to her ankles, slipped off the shoes and stepped clear.

To his further embarrassment, Christopher felt himself becoming aroused. There was a seat against the wall into which he slid as nonchalantly as possible. As she bent over, he could see that she needed to lose some weight off her bottom and thighs. Even he could tell she was not destined for a career as a glamour model unless she slimmed down. She did, however, seem to exude a powerful sexuality.

"Right…I want you to just slowly undress in front of the camera…pretend I'm your boyfriend and you're doing a sexy strip for me, okay? I'll tell you when to stop."

Christopher picked up a magazine that was lying under the chair and pretended to scrutinise its contents. But in reality he couldn't keep his eyes off the girl. As the bra was tossed aside, the strain on the fabric of his underpants was almost too much to bear and he was forced to put the magazine on his lap. When she was naked Harry asked him to help move a couch for her to lie on.

"Yeah…sure," he rose with difficulty, holding the magazine strategically. Noticing this Alison giggled;

Harry raised his eyebrows:

"I think he likes you love."

"For fuck's sake, Harry!" he felt his face reddening.

The couch was positioned and she draped herself over it, in various positions as Harry snapped away.

"Great…great. Right love…I think that'll do. You were great…a real pro. I'll get these developed and if you can come next Wednesday, say, we'll go through them."

"Okay, thanks Harry," she looked at Christopher, naked, hands on hips, "well, have I got what it takes?"

He watched as she bent forward to pull on her knickers and tights, breasts swinging.

"Oh…I guess…"

"Well love, look, come and sit down. I see a lot of girls, as you know, and your body, well, its sexy, very sexy but…"

"Bum and thighs too big!" she cut in.

"Well, as you've put it so bluntly, love…yes. But…a perfect body isn't everything in this business…and who's to say what's a perfect body anyway?…one man's meat (if you'll excuse the expression). You've got to have sex appeal though, if you see what I mean...and you've got that. No question. See what you did to Chris," he slapped him on the back. Christopher looked down at the floor.

"It's just that you may have to diversify, so to speak...do something a little more racey, more daring than, say, Christopher's mag would accommodate."

"You mean spread my legs."

"Well, yeah...are you a Yorkshire lass?"

"No...no, why?"

"Well, you seem to know what's what...you speak your mind...no crap."

They laughed.

"Now, what about videos? Ever thought about being a movie star?"

"What, just stripping...or actual sex?"

"Whatever."

"Well...stripping's okay but I couldn't have sex with someone I didn't know. I mean...I wouldn't mind doing it with a friend..."

"That's fine...fine. But we're jumping the gun. We'll have a look at the prints on Wednesday and see where we go from there."

"Would I get more for video work?"

"Oh yeah, yeah...absolutely, particularly if you were prepared to have sex on camera. There's always a market...particularly in Britain where, strictly, it's still not legal."

"Okay, well I'll think about it and see you on Wednesday. Same time...about 2?"

"That's fine, love. Look, Chris..." he glanced at his watch, "God, is that the time? I've got to go. Call over tomorrow, Chris. After lunch."

"Sure."

He followed Alison up the spiral staircase amazed that he was not able to resist looking up her skirt despite having seen her naked minutes before.

She turned, looked down at him:

"What happened to your hand, Chris?"

"Oh…it's a long story…"

Who's Tarkovsky?

✿ ✿

It was raining steadily when they got outside. Harry pulled the door shut.

"I'd give you a lift but I'm going the opposite way…to Exmouth."

"Doesn't matter Harry…there's a train in half an hour."

"Okay love…see you later Chris."

His car was parked off the main road at the end of the cobbled alleyway that led into the churchyard.

"Fancy a drink?" Christopher nodded in the direction of the pub just across the road.

"It's not open."

"Oh God, no! Of course, it's a bit early."

They backed away from the exhaust of Harry's car.

"Well…um…I've got a chilled bottle of Sauvignon here from Harry's fridge. My place is just down the Strand."

"Oh no…thanks…I should go."

"Come on…we're getting wet. I could find you a few names and addresses…contacts…" he stopped short, ashamed.

"Oh really? Okay then. I could always catch a later train, I suppose."

He made small talk about the Dutch influence on the architecture of the Strand as they walked. His flat was accessed by a flight of steps to a balcony containing two doors…one his, the other his neighbour's. Unlocking the door he pushed against the mound of junk mail with his leading foot and switched on the light. It was cold inside and felt as if it hadn't been lived-in for some time.

"Is this the loo?" she indicated to her left.

"Yes, I'll get some glasses and put the heating on," taking the next left into the kitchen.

He heard the toilet being flushed and the sound of her shoes on the bare floorboards as she made her way into the sitting-room. Pulling open the hatch in the wall, he watched her standing and enjoying the view up-river.

"Splendid sunsets…on a nice evening, of course."

Droplets of rain ran down the windows.

"I should imagine so. This is um…nice. A bit minimal though," she turned to survey the room looking for something that might change her opinion. There was nothing. The furniture consisted of two 'director's' chairs with 'TRUFFAUT' and 'TARKOVSKY' stencilled across the back straps, a nondescript coffee table, a television and video player on a moveable stand and, incongruously, a huge vase, filled with dry pampas grass, located under an open-plan staircase that led up to the next floor.

"It's a maisonette, really," she observed.

"I…I guess it is…yes. Um…do take a seat. Here are the glasses."

As an afterthought, he held one to his nose. It smelt musty so he flushed them under the tap.

She was still standing when he came into the room and set the bottle and glasses on the table. Dust rising from the varnished floorboards swirled around his feet. Gesturing towards the chairs:

"Truffaut or Tarkovsky?"

"Who's Tarkovsky?" she asked.

16

❀ ❀

The bedroom window looked out onto the Strand; street and house lights bright in the gloom. He reached into a cupboard at the top of the stairs and brought out some clean linen:

"Feel a little damp but I guess they'll be okay."

A double mattress lay against one of the walls...the only item of furniture in the room.

"You certainly don't care too much for interior decoration, do you," she observed, giggling...slightly drunk.

He let the mattress fall on the bare floor causing dust to billow into the air.

"Sorry...I'm only here once or twice a year."

She laughed, helping to spread the sheet over the mattress and tucking it underneath.

"Pillows...pillows," he thought aloud then disappeared into the spare room returning with three and a hefty blanket. He put the finishing touches to the bed as she stood back and watched:

"Nice arse!"

"Oh...hah!...thank-you," he sounded surprised. Indeed he couldn't ever recall a woman saying that to him before. It made him self-conscious, embarrassed despite the drink. Perhaps women felt this way when being appraised by men...he couldn't blame them if they did. Reaching forward, as he was bending over with his back towards her, she ran her hand along the inside of his thigh.

"Ohh…watch my hand," he collapsed onto the mattress, spinning round and holding his arm aloft. She jumped on top of him, laughing:

"I like to be in control."

"Be my guest," his voice barely audible.

17

❀ ❀

He was out of breath. Even though she had done most of the work, he somehow felt drained. Leaning back against the pillows, he pulled the light cord. The room became semi-dark. Light filtered through the window highlighting her hair and the bare skin of her arm as she lay with her back towards him.

"Alison...I have a confession..."

"Hmmm," she moved slightly and turned to face him. Her perfume, mingling with the smell of sex and the warmth from her body, made him feel drunk with a glorious sense of well-being. Life suddenly seemed so very simple. It was as if the scattered pieces of a mosaic had come together to form a picture...an answer. As a result, he wanted to hold her so close and so tight that they would completely absorb one another. But it was confession time:

"I...I...don't have any connections."

"What?"

"I don't know anyone in the business. Harry lied... and I went along with it...I'm sorry."

He felt her stiffen. The answers and the questions rapidly parted company. The pieces of the mosaic scattered chaotically.

"You bastard!"

She was standing above him now...poised. He could see her breasts in light and shade, nipples hard with the cold, pointing accusingly. She seemed to relax and then he felt the first warm drops splattering onto his abdomen followed by a cascade over his chest and neck. His first impulse was to seek evasive action but he just lay there, propped against the pillows, breathing in the heady mix of ammonia, sex and perfume, allowing her to take her revenge, laughing like a maniac.

He needn't have worried about the damp sheets after all.

18

❀ ❀

"You fucking enjoyed that, didn't you! You... pervert!"

Mad with rage, she leapt off the bed and ran into the bathroom, slamming the door behind her. He just sat there, unable to control his laughter.

"Alison!" he knocked on the door, cold urine dripping onto the floor forming little puddles around his feet. He could hear the shower, "Alison... I'm sorry. Please let me in."

No reply. He went downstairs and flung his coat around himself, shivering. Hearing the bolt slide, and the door open, he ran back upstairs. She was dressing in the bedroom.

"Sorry," he mumbled, and, turning his back, went into the bathroom and under the still running shower.

When he emerged, ten minutes later, she had gone, leaving the front door open...cold air streaming in from outside.

He stripped the bed and turned the mattress but patches of damp had come through to the other side. Leaning it against the wall, he went back downstairs...bare feet slopping on bare boards. Pushing both chairs together to form a makeshift couch, he huddled into his coat and, watching the headlights of the cars crossing the Exe bridge on the M5, drifted off to sleep.

19

❀ ❀

He was awoken by a sharp pain in his side.

"Oh God…!"

He'd slept, contorted, in the chairs. It took several minutes before he could lift his legs and place his feet on the floor. Gingerly, he straightened up, grimacing, flexing his back as it lost its stiffness. His watch showed 10.53. The sun was shining across the river, highlighting the hills beyond. The windshield of a boat, moored on the water, reflected its light…flash…flash…moving with the current, back and forth.

Food. He was starving. There was nothing, of course, not even a tin of beans.

"Fuck!"

He mounted the stairs…carefully…dressed quickly in the previous days' clothes and was about to retrace his steps when the doorbell rang. Thinking it was Alison, he ran to the door, called:

"Hang on, will you," in his grumpiest voice, before relieving himself in the toilet nearby thinking: 'she can bloody well wait!'

He heard a man clearing his throat, saw the letterbox open, heard his voice:

"Mr Purbright? Mr Christopher Purbright?"

"Yeah, yeah…hang on. Who is it? Oh damn…"

Surprised, he had jerked away from the toilet bowl and re-anointed his feet:

'Well, I suppose at least it's my own piss,' he thought.

"My name is Harris, sir, Detective Superintendent Harris."

20

❀ ❀

"I'm Detective Superintendent Harris…my identification. This is Policewoman Shaw."

Christopher glanced at the card, then at the policewoman. Her face, he thought, was vaguely familiar—maybe he had seen her around the town.

"May we come in, sir? There are a few questions I need to ask you."

Christopher stood aside:

"Oh, yes…yes…sorry. I've just woken up. Please excuse me…what's this all about?"

They pushed past him as he closed the door.

"Um…take a seat…please…" he gestured towards the directors' chairs. The policewoman removed her hat to reveal a heavily restrained head of brown hair. She chose Truffaut and, when seated, pulled a notebook and pen from a briefcase.

"Tarkovsky…great director, sir," said Harris, "I liked the one where that actor takes ten minutes to walk the length of an emptied swimming-pool. Has to keep going back because his candle blows out."

"Um…oh…yes...*Nostalgia*," Christopher seated himself on the window ledge, facing them both.

"That's the one, sir. Beautifully filmed...an artist, Tarkovsky, sir, an artist who paints on celluloid. You can take a frame from any one of his films, stick it on the wall, and it would look perfect...just perfect. But, alas, much too slow and thoughtful for today's *Pulp Fiction* audience."

"Yes…yes," Christopher nodded and smiled. It wasn't every day that he met someone who had even heard of Tarkovsky, let alone seen his films. His natural inclination to continue the conversation was curbed by the circumstances. He looked expectantly at the burly policeman who was, he thought, probably in his mid-fifties, having an unruly but healthy head of greying hair. His eyes seemed small but this was due to an habitual squint which Christopher found somewhat unnerving, fearing it to be the result of a lifetime of doubt and suspicion rather than myopia.

"So…well, it's about Alison Moltby, sir. You've no doubt heard…"

"Alison!…what's happened to her? I mean…she was only here last night!"

Harris and Shaw both stood up:

"What?" a gold tooth glinted as his mouth gaped open.

"Well…yes…I mean…she left a few hours ago. We…um…had a disagreement…"

"A disagreement? Well, where did she go?" he looked around as if expecting to see her under the stairs.

"Well…home, I presume. Although at that time she would have had to call a taxi, I guess."

"Taxi?" his brow furrowed and his eyes squinted… seriously perplexed. He stared beyond Christopher, up-river, then sat down again:

"Are you saying that Alison was here…last night?"

"Well, yes…someone called Alison was here. I don't know her surname but I presume it's her you're talking about. Will you please tell me what has happened to her?"

Harris turned his head slightly to one side and squinted at him through his left eye:

"And…um…how old was this *Alison*, sir?"

"Oh…nineteen…twenty, possibly."

"Ahhhh…," he nodded his head sagely, "not the Alison *we're* looking for, sir…obviously. Does the name Alison *Moltby* not mean anything to you?"

He looked down at this point and spotted the newspaper lying on the floor where Christopher had left it the previous evening:

"Have you read this?"

"No…no…I've not heard of an Alison Moltby. Should I have?"

He unfolded the paper and held open the front page:

'ALISON: HOUSE TO HOUSE ENQUIRIES'

"Can't believe you don't know about it, sir."

"Well, you see, I don't live here. I live in Nottingham most of the time. Travelled down yesterday. Not really seen any news. Bought that last night but didn't have time to look at it."

"Ah…well…she's a nine year old schoolgirl. Missing since Wednesday night."

"Oh dear. I'm sorry…but what's it got to do with me?"

21

❀ ❀

"Well, sir," eyebrows raised, "don't you recognise the name? We've been trying to contact you since Thursday."

Christopher screwed up his face, threw his arms wide in a gesture of defeat and shrugged:

"But I've never heard of her!"

Harris furrowed his brow again:

"Really? And what about her mother...Nancy?"

"Nancy?" he was still none the wiser.

"Nancy Moltby...was an...um...exotic dancer at the Riverwalk Club...in Exeter."

"Nancy!"

"So you do know her?"

"Well...yes...yes...must be getting on towards ten years since I saw her"

He slumped against the window pane.

"Nancy...gosh...I've lost touch. So she had a kid?"

Harris's lower jaw fell:

"Well...yes...indeed she did, sir! Yours... apparently!"

"What!" he stood up and stared wide-eyed at Harris, then at policewoman Shaw, as if challenging her to contradict what had been said. She looked down and shifted uncomfortably in her chair, clearly embarrassed.

"You...um...didn't know then, sir?"

"No...no...I..." he tailed off, lost for words.

"She said as much. But we had to check it out...make sure, like."

"But...why didn't she tell me? And...uh...why me? How does she know it's mine? She was flaunting it every night at the club. Punters were eating out of her hands. She could have had anyone she wanted…everyone she wanted. Must have had hundreds of lovers…surely?"

"But she didn't…or so she says. Now, sir," he got up and removed his overcoat, placing it over the back of the chair and walking up to the window, hands in the jacket pockets of a very nondescript suit.

Christopher had sat down again, head in hands. Harris was speaking but the words did not penetrate.

"I'm…I'm sorry Inspector…I'm just shocked, you know. You must give me a moment to collect my thoughts."

"Of course, of course," he laid a hand on his shoulder, "why doesn't Policewoman Shaw here make us all a nice cup of coffee."

"Oh…I'm sorry…I only arrived last night. There's nothing here…sorry…not even coffee."

"Well…just get him a drink of water then."

"No, no…it's alright. I'll be okay…thank-you…Um… I'd better go and see her, I guess. Do you know where she lives?"

"Of course…she wants to see you. Said you'd have nothing to do with all this business but…you understand …we really do need to ask you a few questions. To eliminate you from our enquiries, as they say."

"Yeah…yeah…of course."

Harris looked down and frowned:

"What happened to your hand?"

22

✾ ✾

"When was the last time you saw Nancy Moltby?"

"Well...as I said...it must have been...ten...years ago. I'd just sold my parents' house on Mamouth Street and bought this...then moved up to Nottingham. I come back regularly but have not seen her since. I was joint owner of the Club, you know. She lived nearby in Okehampton Street. We often went back to her place...in the early hours...after the Club had closed for the night."

"How long did this arrangement last?"

"Oh, couple of months...that's all. Then one night we had a row and she told me to fuck off. And I haven't seen her since."

"And you say you didn't know about the baby?"

"No...no...absolutely not. I just sold my share in the club to help buy my house in Nottingham. Haven't been back there since."

"You sold out to Gerard Anthony?"

"Yes...yes...Gerard. Have you spoken to him? Oh, of course you have...silly of me."

Again the eyes squinted:

"And what is your opinion of Mr Anthony?"

"Gerard? Well, I knew his son at school. But then he went on to University and we lost touch. But I bumped into Gerard in the library...the big one...in town...Castle Street. We had lunch and he mentioned he was raising cash to buy this nightclub. Seemed like a good investment."

"So you never really got to know him then?"

"Not socially. Strictly business."

"And the Club? Was everything above board?"

"What do you mean?"

"Well, you sold your share. Were you unhappy with the way it was being run?"

"No...no...I told you. I wanted to buy this house in Nottingham. Wanted to move away."

"Yes, you said. I just thought that maybe something upset you..."

"Oh...what do you mean? Something illegal? Drugs?"

"Possibly...or...prostitution...pornography or, even," he curled his upper lip, the tooth glinted, "paedophilia?"

Christopher jumped to his feet:

"Good God, no...nothing like that! Not at all. It was just girls stripping...nothing more sinister than that."

"I see. And could you tell me where you were last Wednesday...when the girl disappeared?"

Christopher looked perplexed:

"Um...Wednesday...I was at home...in Nottingham."

"Anyone corroborate that?"

"Um...no...not really...my cat, Brocard?"

"I'm afraid it would have to be someone we could speak to, sir."

"I'm sorry...there is no one. I stayed in all day."

He turned and picked up his coat.

"Well, thank-you for your time, Mr Purbright. Could I ask you to keep us posted as to your whereabouts?"

"Oh...I'm staying put here for a while."

"Good, good...oh, here's Mrs Moltby's number," he ripped out a page from a notebook taken from the inside pocket of his jacket, "it's an Exeter number. She's staying with friends. It's best, in these cases, to keep her away from the Press…you understand. Please don't give the number to anyone else."

"I won't. Thank-you."

He glanced at the policewoman as she passed—hazel eyes, thin sensuous lips, slightly up-turned nose:

"Do I know you from somewhere?"

She smiled:

"I'm Penelope Shaw. You went to school with my sister, Christine."

"Christine! Of course! You look just like her…um…a younger version, of course. Do you still live locally?"

"Exeter."

"Hmmm…well give my regards to Christine when you see her."

She smiled…there was a glint in her eyes:

"I'm afraid she's in Australia. Moved out there about twelve years ago. Married a professor of something or the other. Don't see much of her these days."

"Really? Oh…well…good for her!"

"You're a literary man aren't you, Mr Purbright?" Harris was squinting at him again.

"Yes…yes I've written a few things."

"Yes, indeed. I remember all the fuss about that novel of yours. A few people around here didn't take too kindly to it, I understand."

"Well, you could say that. I thought attitudes might have changed a little since I left. But there still appears to be some right-wing reactionaries here, living in a previous century, I'm afraid."

"That's as maybe, sir. Haven't read it myself. Poetry's my forté. Speaking of which—do you know a Mr Lethbridge-Wright?"

"Name rings a bell."

"Lives up on Mamouth Street."

"Oh yes, yes…of course…bought my parents old house off me."

"Really? Small world! Um…you wouldn't happen to know where he is, by any chance?"

"No idea. Never actually met him. The sale was conducted through his solicitor."

"Oh…well, anyway, he's a poet…published, like yourself."

"Really?…small world."

"Indeed it is, sir," they reached the door which Policewoman Shaw was having difficulty opening. Christopher pushed past, placing a hand on her waist. Upon contact, a tingling sensation, like static electricity, passed along his fingers and up his arm causing him to withdraw his hand. He looked at her quizzically and she just smiled obviously unaware of his discomfort. He fumbled with the catch on the door and after a little persuasion it opened. A blast of cold air made him shiver.

"Thank you again, sir, good-day," Harris stepped out after Penelope Shaw. He watched her walk away— Christine Shaw's sister!

Memories came flooding back. Her body, despite the uniform (or maybe because of it) looked as slim, firm and pleasing as he remembered her sister's had been.

All those years ago. Another blast of cold air brought him to his senses.

He shivered again and closed the door.

Quickly ascending the stairs, he crossed to the bedroom window and watched Harris and Penelope Shaw climb into a car parked in the courtyard.

He felt uneasy.
Could he really be a father…?

23

Christopher turned his back, leaned against the sill and slid his hands down over his face, as if hoping that by doing so it would somehow turn back the clock half an hour, making everything that had been said unsaid.

Nancy! A child...*his* child. No...it couldn't be possible. He sat on the stairs staring blankly at the view up-river without taking anything in.

Mental calculations...

Associations...

Dates...

Places...

Names...

Memories…

Yes, it must have been ten years ago. The girl was nine, they said. Well, that checks, at least. But surely she had more lovers than him?

Happy Shopper
❀ ❀

He glanced at the piece of notepaper in his hand. Too early to ring. Best to go up the town and get some provisions. His stomach grumbled in agreement. Ensuring his wallet and keys were in his jacket pocket, he left the flat. Reaching the bottom of the steps, he turned left into the Strand, then left again toward the shopping centre. There was a time, he mused, when he'd have only needed to walk 50 yards to the nearest grocery shop. Thirty years ago, maybe less, there was a shop at the bottom of Mamouth Street, where it met Mamouth Hill, the steep incline off the Strand that he was now passing. But now the nearest shop for provisions was mid-town, on Fore Street, the Co-op. Quite a trek. The Lighter Inn, at the end of the Strand, advanced towards him. A single-decker bus flashed by in front of it, terminating on the Quay to his left, turning around for the return journey to Exeter.

He hardly registered any of this, even though it was all there for him to see, there was too much going on inside his head. It all seemed so unreal. He was a father…maybe. And his daughter was missing…abducted…perhaps dead. He may have gained and lost a daughter in one day! Call the Guinness Book of Records!

The pavements of this old town were narrow. He had to constantly step off to allow others to pass. Spotting a teashop, he hurried inside ordering two waffles and a cup of coffee without waiting for the waitress to call at his table. The place was deserted and he was served quickly. The waffles, smothered in maple syrup, disappeared rapidly and he ordered two more. He could feel the energy levels in his body rise and with them his spirits.

'Look after the body,' he thought, 'and then the mind can expand.'

A warm glow enveloped him and, taking a deep breath, he felt, for a second, immortal. As he paid his bill and left, it was as if he were walking on air. The colours on the packets in the supermarket looked brighter and more attractive than usual. He bought more as a result but didn't really mind. All was well. And as he emptied his bags, filling the fridge and one of the cupboards in his flat with colour, he thanked whatever deity was responsible for his existence that day.

Then he remembered Nancy...

25

"Could I speak to Nancy, please?"

"Who wants her?"

"Nancy? It's Chris…um…Christopher…"

"Oh! Have the police seen you?"

"Yeah…yeah, they gave me your number. Um…listen …can this be true? I mean…?"

"You'd better come and see me. We can't speak on the phone."

"Yes, of course, where are you?"

"Staying with a friend…Natasha…remember her?"

"Um…," unsure, "look…*is this true*? Yes or no? I need to know! Am I the father of this kid?"

Pause.

"Yes…yes you are…"

"What!"

"Look, just come round and see me. I'm at 50 Raymond Road…near St Leonard's church."

"Yeah…yeah…I know it. But…"

The line went dead.

"Fuck!"

26

※ ※

The shop at the bottom of Raymond Road, like so many other corner shops, had gone. Christopher's aunt had lived here, twenty, thirty years ago. The road curved to the right and rose steeply with rows of terraced houses on either side. Number 50 was half way up on the right. The outer door was propped open with a brick. He knocked on the glass of the inner door. Natasha, an overweight but still attractive blond woman in her early thirties, answered.

"Oh...Christopher," a throaty voice, "lovely to see you. I'm Natasha...do you remember me?"

"Of course," it was all coming back, " how are you?"

"Fine...fine. Not at the Club anymore. I work at Dimbleby's store in town."

"Make-up department?" he said it without thinking.

"Yeah...how did you guess?"

Her face resembled a plaster cast. If she laughed too heartily, he thought, it might crack open.

"Uh...I guess Nancy must have said."

"Yeah...anyway...I don't think many punters would pay to see me naked these days. Put too much weight on." Stepping to the right and into a room that led to the kitchen, she swung around, put her hands on her hips and thrust her shoulders back. She had, indeed, put on weight...everywhere, he thought.

"You look great to me, Tash."

"Go on!" she laughed, "tea?"

"Ugh...no thanks. Got any wine?"

"Sorry...orange juice?"

"Oh...no thanks. Where's Nancy?"

"Oh...she had to go out. Wouldn't be long, she said. Gerard picked her up."

"Gerard?"

"Gerard Anthony."

"Oh...Gerard...of course. I've been away, you know... living in Nottingham. Lost touch. Is the club still going then?"

"Yeah...oh yeah. Nancy still works there. She's pretty hot for her age...hasn't let herself go...not like me."

"Tash, you look great. I remember the punters really liked you..."

"Hah," throaty laugh, "not as much as Nance; especially when she wore that schoolgirl uniform and shaved her pubes."

"And the tennis skirt!"

"Oh...oh yeah, they went wild for that!"

"Hmmm...and didn't you used to borrow blokes' spectacles..."

"Yeah...slipped the crook of the arm inside my knickers then put them back on the punter. I remember one dirty old bloke who used to take them off again and lick them...," again the throaty laugh, "there's a video somewhere...upstairs maybe. That guy...Harry Whatis-name...Yorkshire bloke..."

"Ollershaw?"

"Yeah, that's him. He was always at the Club filming us."

"When did you leave?

"Couple of years after you went. Nancy had the baby and then went back but by then I'd had enough."

"Oh?"

"Yeah," she crinkled her nose, "I don't know…it just wasn't the same. There were some funny people hanging around…upstairs mostly. Gerard had some executive suites put in…with one-way glass. Girls could earn a bit extra if one of the punters liked her act…know what I mean? I got lots of offers but always turned them down. Gerard didn't like that. Tried to pressurize me. It got a bit heavy so I left."

"And Nancy's baby…did *you* know it was mine?"
She looked away:

"She told me but I'd already guessed. She didn't go with anyone else at that time…just you…I would have known…she always told me everything about her blokes."

"But…"

"She said it was yours and I was not to tell anybody. Except…well…when she disappeared, like, she thought you might have guessed and made off with her so she told the Police. You haven't, have you…made off with her?"

"What! No! I had no idea…and even if I had…I mean…why didn't she tell me?"

"Oh, you'd gone…and anyway…she wanted the kid to herself."

"Shit!" in exasperation, "I can't believe this!"

"I'm sorry, love," she placed her hand on his arm, "if this hadn't have happened nobody would have been any the wiser."

"Great!" sarcastically.

"Sorry, love…that was thoughtless. Look…sit down. Make yourself comfortable. Nancy won't be long, I'm sure," she motioned towards some comfortable chairs arranged around a blocked-off fireplace.

"Um…," embarrassed, "shall I get that video. We could watch it whilst you're waiting. Relive old times, like."

"Whatever…"

"Come through to the sitting room."

This room, adjacent to the other, had a sash window overlooking the road. There was just enough room for a comfortable-looking three-piece-suite and a large wide-screen television. Magazines were strewn over the furniture and the remnants of a takeaway littered the floor.

"Sorry about the mess."

There was a knock at the door.

"Who the fuck's that!" more of an challenge than a question, "sorry."

She bounded out of the room leaving Christopher to clear a space on the sofa before sitting down.

Muffled voices:

"What do *you* want?"

A hesitant male voice:

"I…I was just passing…and…and I wondered…"

"Well don't! You should ring and make an appointment. How dare you!"

"I…I'm sorry…I was just passing and I thought…"

"Well don't! Now go away and don't bother me. I have someone here."

"Oh…" he sounded crestfallen but stood his ground as if expecting her to change her mind.

"An old friend…"

"I could wait upstairs. I'd be very quiet…please?" it was almost pitiful.

"Go away! Call me tonight," the door slammed.

She re-entered the room head lowered, sheepishly:

"When I said that I worked at Dimbleby's, it was only partially true. I work there part-time but I also entertain men…and women…who like to be dominated. Upstairs."

"Oh…was this Gerard's idea?"

"No…mine. Business is good," again the throaty laugh.

"Hmmm, obviously, if they feel the need to visit without an appointment."

"Oh…him? He always does that. He knows I'll be particularly hard on him if he dares to call on spec."

"Well…I hadn't ever thought of you as a dominatrix, Natasha!"

"Oh, its amazing how convincing you can be if you know the person you are with *wants* to be convinced."

"I suppose so."

"What did you do to your hand?"

"Oh…dislocated a finger."

"Ugh! Is it painful?"

"It's okay now. Will be able to take this off soon."

"Good. How did you manage…?"

He raised his hand:

"Don't ask."

"Okay…I'll get the video."

27

✿ ✿

Christopher left the house, quietly, before she returned. It came to him, all too painfully, that to watch Nancy dancing in that costume—the tennis skirt, tee-shirt and the racquet which she rubbed between her legs—stripping, going through her act, working the audience, and him, with consummate skill and control, would be too much for him to bear.

Outside the door, he turned right, crossed the road and took the first left. A few minutes later he was on the Western Way, heading for Paris Street, deep in thought, immersed in the past. It had struck him, forcefully, for the first time, that Nancy's lovemaking had been little more than an extension of her act. She had often worn that tennis skirt in bed, called all the shots, rode him as he lay passively beneath her. He had loved it, of course, and her…yes…he had loved her and thought himself loved in return. She could have had anyone but she chose him. He fell under her spell. And all the time she was…well …milking him. If she had just told him…come clean right from the start…he might not have allowed himself to fall in love so pitifully. He could have relaxed and just enjoyed the sex without strings. She wanted the baby but not the father—the rejection was mortifying. He remembered the events of the day she had broken off their relationship with such clarity that it all could have happened yesterday. The film was all there, loaded onto the projector, ready to re-run, inside his head. He'd closed and locked the door of the projection room some time ago but now he had the key in his hand and he watched himself staggering out of her flat, heading for the Paris Street bus station, as indeed, he was now. There he had boarded the Plymouth bus, alighting at Bovey Tracey on the south-eastern fringe of Dartmoor where a mini-bus took him to Widecombe-in-the-Moor. From there he had tramped up the steep lane to Hamel Down, a vast ridge high above the world. On Hamel Down Tor he had stood among the rocks, hair streaming in the wind, hoping it would clear all the clutter that had accumulated in his head over the years…trying to blow her away.

As he had gazed out over the vast moorland with the snake-like road below and the prehistoric settlement of Grimspound laid before him, he gained a sense of perspective. For this was where nature and history conspired to make everything else unimportant. Nothing could touch him here, except the elements…this was Dartmoor…the equaliser…

Dartmoor

❀ ❀

…and it looked exactly the same as he stood there once again, having arrived by the same route.

Tears welled-up in his eyes; a bitter wind stung his face, chilled his body, reminding him that he was not properly dressed for rambling.

He huddled behind a rock and looked up at the sky where small white clouds scurried after each other, occasionally blotting out the late afternoon sun. Another two or three hours and it would be dark—time to make a move.

He gazed down at the remains of the prehistoric settlement of Grimspound, situated in the valley between the two tors. A number of hut circles could be seen from this height surrounded by the remains of what must have been a thick double wall built in the Middle Bronze Age not for defence, obviously, but simply to keep animals and people in. The moor was probably heavily wooded in those days and almost certainly a lot warmer than now— warm enough to grow crops. So the trees were felled, the land tilled and then, many years later, when the climate changed and the people left for the warmer valleys, Dartmoor became a wilderness. He smirked—far from being unspoilt, this was truly a man-made environment. But because his ancestors had made a success of survival here, he was able to stand, thousands of years later, and look down at the homes where they had lived and died. Maybe that was why he was so drawn to this site and always kept it in his mind. It was like coming home. There was a clear sense of Mankind's beginning here and also, it seemed to him, It's end.

Thinking these thoughts, he commenced the long descent but did not walk through the settlement by way of the piled rocks that formed the entrance, choosing instead to strike off in the direction of Hound Tor where he would meet the minibus that would return him to civilisation. But first a cross-country trek to Natsworthy Manor, past Jay's Grave always mysteriously be-decked with flowers. Here a curious feeling of depression passed over him and he pushed on towards the Tor, an eerie landmark which had featured in various film adaptations of *The Hound of the Baskervilles*. But before he reached this, he heard the minibus behind him and flagged it down. Ten minutes later he was back in Bovey Tracey and checking into the Devon Hotel for the night.

Katie May
❀ ❀

After his meal he retired to the bar. A young girl—she looked barely old enough to be in a bar—caught his eye and smiled. He looked away but she was at his table in an instant:

"Boi us a drink, maister?" the accent was broad Devonshire. He could scarcely understand what she was saying.

"What would you like?"

"Zider, if 'e plaze."

Glancing back from the bar, he studied her appearance: shoulder-length black dishevelled hair (needed brushing); clothes (not in vogue)—a cotton blouse partially covered by a cardigan with missing buttons, a skirt that came to her knees, no tights underneath (nor socks), shoes in need of repair.

"Do you live in Bovey?" he asked, setting the cider in front of her.

"O no! Oi lives in a varm...up on moor."

"So what are you doing here?"

"Drinkin'…jus' drinkin'."

"Do you have any money?"

"O ar, oi got money okay. An' a car. Wanna come for a droive?"

"You can drive?" he laughed.

"What's vunny 'bout that?"

"Well, you look scarcely old enough."

"Oi'm twenny-two!" indignantly.

"You never are?"

"I bloody is too!" she pouted, distinctly hurt.

The cheeks reddened on her rounded face. Dimples appeared then disappeared as she tensed and relaxed. Her eyes, black and sparkling, fixed on his, pulling him in.

"U come fer a droive. Oi'll show 'e."

Unable to resist, he rose to his feet, and leaving the drinks untouched, followed her out into the night, watching the slender hips move from side to side as she walked.

The car, a Morris Minor splashed with mud, was parked in a side street.

Throwing back her head, she laughed as she drove him out of town and up onto the moor, pointing out Hay Tor, Saddle Tor, Rippon Tor, the road to Widdecombe, Honeybag, Chinkwell and Hound Tors. Soon after that she fell silent, her face pale and drawn in the reflected dashboard light. Before he could speak she turned onto a dirt track and stopped the car outside a farmhouse with granite walls and a thatched roof. Reaching over she kissed him full on the lips, gently brushing the inside of his thigh with her hand.

He swallowed hard:

"I...I don't know your name?"

"Katie...Katie May," and raising her eyebrows she turned and stepped from the car.

"Wait 'ere 'til oi've gone inside. Then come. Bring the torch," she indicated towards the glove compartment. He watched her hips sway in the headlight beam.

To his surprise she didn't go into the farmhouse but continued a little farther to an outbuilding. Opening the door, she beckoned to him. He took the torch and followed, switching off the headlights.

The door was closed when he reached it. Lifting the latch, he aimed the torch inside. The beam of light illuminated her body, which hung by the neck from a rope slung across a beam, swaying gently back and forth …creaking like a child's garden swing. He froze, dropped the torch, cried out and woke up in his hotel room in Bovey Tracey, bedside lamp knocked to the floor, streetlight outside filtering through the curtains…orange. Wiping the sweat from his face, he crossed to the window. It was 2 a.m. by his watch.

A car engine started up in the side street next to the hotel. He watched as a mud-splattered Morris Minor pulled out onto the road and headed off in the direction of the moor.

30a

❀ ❀

The next day he caught the early bus to Lustleigh—a small village three miles away on the fringe of the moor. Here began one of his favourite walks—Lustleigh Cleave, the Bovey and Becka valleys, Becka Falls. He should have felt full of the joy and anticipation of the open road but the memory of his dream hung around him like an overcoat. He felt oppressed, haunted by a sense of doom. Kitty Jay, the suicide buried at the crossroads near Hound Tor had, indeed, according to legend, hung herself at a nearby farm. He knew the story well but at no time during his dream did he sense that he was participating in a latter-day re-enactment. There was a pain above and between his eyes—a tension accumulated during the night and stubbornly refusing to disperse. His stomach rumbled, reminding him that he had skipped breakfast at the hotel in order to catch the bus. The teashop in the village square probably wouldn't be open yet. Then he remembered Katherine.

Katherine was a novelist, a widow in her early forties who lived in a cottage by the Post Office. They had met, many years previously, on the Cleave. She had been meditating in the sunshine at Sharpitor, sitting cross-legged on the grass. Christopher had been standing nearby, admiring the spectacular view across the valley, when she opened her eyes. They were soon striding along the ridge towards Hunter's Tor, talking. She had taken him back to her cottage and introduced him to her husband—already ailing, it seemed—pale and walking with a stick. She wrote and said he had died a few months later but never specified the nature of his illness.

The bus dropped him at the edge of the village before turning round and heading back toward the main road. He trudged in the direction of the church and stood for a while under its lychgate. In his depression he found himself wondering how many coffins had sheltered there awaiting the arrival of the Minister. The tea-shop was, to his surprise, already open but he turned instead down a side street to where a picturesque thatched cottage stood, in its own grounds, behind a four-foot high granite wall. The gate was broken and propped against a tree-trunk. As he entered the garden several things happened at once: the sun came out, sending a slanting beam of bright light across the scene, highlighting objects and sending others into deep shadow producing the dream-like clarity of a De Chirico painting; the church clock struck, the sound resonating in the still morning air; and a rabbit bounded across the path ahead of him and disappeared through a hole in the hedge. At that moment it seemed to him that time had inexplicably stopped with the chiming of the bell and that only he—and the rabbit—were moving through it in slow motion. And, after what seemed like several minutes, when he finally reached the door of the cottage, he realised that the tension and resulting oppression and doom had lifted, almost exactly like, and as easy as, shedding a layer of clothing. He turned round, took a deep breath and laughed out loud. Glancing to his left, he saw Katherine sitting at the window of her study squinting in his direction, not recognising him at first.

"Christopher!" she mouthed through the glass.

He nodded and smiled.

"Christopher!"

"Katherine!"

They embraced.

"Well, this is a surprise. Why didn't you phone? I might not have been in."

He shrugged.

Her hair, he noticed, once long, black and wavy, was now almost entirely grey and frizzy. But her eyes, bright and brown, were as young as ever albeit underlined with black and crow's feet wrinkles.

"I'll make some tea…"

"Oh, coffee, please, if you have it. And could you spare me some toast?"

"Of course, yes," turning, smiling, "although it will have to be gluten-free bread. I have this allergy, you see. Briony has it too, poor thing. We have to get our bread, vacuum packed, from the pharmacy; but it's not bad toasted."

"How is Briony?"

"She's well. 15 now. Goes to school in Newton Abbot. Has to get up very early in the morning, poor thing, to catch the bus. But it's worth it. Good school."

The kitchen had a stone floor with a solid pine table and benches set at one end against some French windows.

"So, what are you doing in these parts?"

Her hands were busy spooning instant coffee into mugs, pouring on the hot water, waiting for his approval then stirring in cold milk.

"Sugar?"

"No…no thanks…I'm staying in Tapshed awhile. Thought of doing the Cleave today. Need to clear my head."

"Oh, I'd love to join you but I've got to finish this wretched novel. Publishers want it signed sealed and delivered by the end of next week."

"That's okay. I'd prefer to be on my own up there, actually. No offence…I've just got some things to think through."

She nodded, not wishing to intrude, handing him a steaming mug and a plate of toast.

"Come and sit in the study."

They walked through to a room lined with bookshelves. Two comfortable armchairs were arranged around an open fireplace. A solid oak writing desk, covered in papers, occupied the area in front of the window.

"Sit down," she plumped-up one of the cushions on the nearest armchair. He sunk down into it with a sigh. Looking up, after she had made herself comfortable in the chair opposite, their eyes met.

"Well," awkwardly, as is often the case when there is so much to talk about, "how are things with you? What about that bloke you were telling me about?"

"Oh…Brian?" she slapped her forehead in despair, "I was such a fool!"

"But I though you were thinking of re-marrying?"

"Well…yes…but that was before I realised he was an alcoholic."

"Oh…"

"Yes…well…I got him into rehab but then he left and refused to go back. So we went to Vienna for a holiday—me, Briony, him and his two kids. I paid for everything and then—would you believe it—he said he'd come without his wallet! Caught him stealing from my handbag on the last day. He denied it, of course, as all alcoholics do, but..." she trailed off to take a few sips from her cup, "after I'd paid for everything, even his kids' passports."

"Oh Katherine...that's terrible. You've sent him packing, I presume?"

"Oh yeah...now I have but Briony told me all along that he was just using me. A few months ago my bag disappeared from the car—diary, address book, credit cards, cheque book, mobile phone...the lot! Must have been him. It was just one thing after another. I was more like his mother than his partner. It cost me a fortune straightening out his debts; then there were the court hearings with his ex-wife, driving him to rehab, taking him to job interviews...generally helping him sort out his life. But all he's done is let me down time and time again...oh, I'm sorry, Chris, you don't want to hear all this...it's just that when I first met him he was so kind and attentive...just what I needed after...," she trailed off and looked down into her mug.

"Yes...yes...you said in your letters..."

"...he was so much fun to be with. God! What a contrast to last month, when I left him. Moved my stuff out of his flat in Bovey whilst he lay in a drunken stupor. Then he had the gall to keep ringing me up, leaving abusive messages on the answer machine. He even rang the police and accused *me* of stealing from him. Then, a few weeks ago, he drove round here, in the car that I had bought for him, slashed my tyres and kicked the gate off its hinges."

"Did the police do anything?"

"No...no witnesses. He came round in the early hours."

"No, I mean *his* complaint about you?"

"Oh…oh no," she laughed, "he was drunk at 10am when they came to interview him. Told him to stop wasting police time!"

"Well, that's something…is he still hassling you?"

"No, I've had the number changed. Just want to forget him now. He's wasted six months of my life…the bastard!"

She looked at him and smiled. The relief on her face revealed the therapeutic value of his visit.

"I cancelled the insurance for his car to pay for the slashed tyres…so it will serve him right if he has an accident—which is very likely given that he's usually drunk. Must get the gate mended too."

He looked down at the carpet, wishing to change the subject. The remains of a biscuit protruded from under the armchair. For no reason, he pushed it underneath with the heel of his shoe.

"What's the novel about?"

"Oh…another mystery…set here on the moor in the nineteenth century. About Kitty Jay…you know, the girl who killed herself and is buried on the crossroads near Hound Tor."

He knew.

31a

✿ ✿

Feeling refreshed and elated, he bounded over the stile near Hammerslake that led up to the ridge overlooking Lustleigh Cleave. He had sat and listened to Katherine's tale of woe with the utmost objectivity, examining word after word, as if under a microscope, without becoming emotionally involved. Not in any way cold, clinical, unsympathetic but with a warm understanding.

Now, as the sun filtered through the trees, he stopped and took a deep breath. More deep breaths followed as he scrambled up the steep incline. When he reached Sharpitor, with its fine view over the wooded valley below, he felt quite light-headed—on top of the world, master of all he surveyed. The climax of a Sibelius symphony, number 2, spontaneously re-played itself inside his head and a painting by Caspar David Friedrich came to mind—a man, seen from behind, standing on a high ridge, alone. A cool breeze blew through his hair, drying the perspiration on his brow. He rested against a massive block of granite and as he closed his eyes, he experienced that same compression of time he had felt in the garden earlier—yesterday, today, tomorrow all mixed up together, swirling around like water poured into a bucket. And he knew with certainty that, at that moment, he could choose—as if a portal had opened and all he need do was step inside. He hesitated, and with a judder that made his heart palpitate, he was back in the here and now.

The landscape felt alive now as he descended; tall gorse bushes on either side of the path interspersed with the rejuvenating bracken. He felt a kind of vibration coming up from the earth through his feet. His fingers tingled as if conducting an electrical charge.

He reached the valley floor and crossed to the river, watching it hurry by over its bed of granite. A wooden log bridge nearby afforded the only crossing. He removed his shoes and socks and sat there, dangling his feet in the cold clear water, mesmerised. Detritus, carried from the moor, swept beneath the bridge; some, caught in eddies, swirled and became stuck against the bank but most was carried unhindered downstream to where three rivers converged, merged with the Teign and, inevitably, the sea. No sense of time standing still here—the water that rippled through his toes would soon be in the ocean.

Rising, he walked to the far bank and lay there waiting for his feet to dry and before the sound of the water could lull him to sleep, he was scrambling up the pathway that led to the ridge between the Bovey and the Becka valleys. At Becka Falls, where the river cascades about seventy or eighty feet along a rocky bed, there was a café. He was counting on it being open as he was in need of a drink.

The falls were in full flow when he arrived, swollen by the recent rains. Crossing the wooden bridge to the car park, he saw that the café was indeed open—some tourists stood outside drinking from cans.

The elderly man behind the counter looked as if he had always been there, perhaps even constructed the falls himself in his youth, when the world too was young. But when he smiled a welcome, many of the creases on his face melted away, and Christopher was able to estimate his age at mid-sixties, no more. It was mid-afternoon so he ordered a Devonshire cream tea which, for the uninitiated, consists of a pot of tea, two huge scones, strawberry jam and clotted cream. The trick was to remember to spread the jam on the scone first, and then add the cream. If the cream was used first, any locals observing the proceedings would know immediately that you were 'not from these parts'. Christopher, of course, requested coffee. His host replied sarcastically,

"One Devonshire cream tea...with coffee."

There were half a dozen wooden benches on the grass outside. He asked for his tray to be brought to him. Sitting down, he laid his head on the table, closed his eyes and relaxed. His body tingled from exertion and his clothes stuck wherever they touched his perspiring body. Taking some deep breaths and expelling the air slowly, he felt his body cool down. The cold wood against his cheek was pleasant and when he turned to cool the other, he opened his eyes and saw a young woman walking toward him holding a tray. His eyes opened wide...she had bright red shoulder-length hair, obviously dyed. Her face and arms were milky white and, he noticed as she came closer, slightly freckled. Mouth wide, lips full and as red as her hair, teeth white, eyes green, eyebrows dark and thick. There was a gold ring through her left nostril. She was wearing a mint green sleeveless vest and powder blue trousers. He couldn't speak. As she set the tray in front of him he tried to smile but she was already walking away.

As he ate and drank, he couldn't take his mind off her until two large ferocious-looking geese appeared from behind the building and waddled menacingly in his direction. The object of their attention—as he soon learned—was the half-eaten scone on his plate which they seemed to think was theirs by right. Standing intimidatingly to either side of him they hissed and snapped at his forearms and hands. The red-haired woman came running:

"I'm so sorry. They're always doing that—the gate wasn't locked properly," there was a trace of a Devonshire accent in her voice which education had concealed but not eradicated.

"Are you from around here?" he managed to say.

"Bovey…I live with my granddad."

"Oh…I'm staying in Bovey. At the Devon Hotel."

"Oh…you a tourist then?"

She was shooing the geese; he was pretending to help but kept a safe distance.

"No…not really. I live over near Exeter, Tapshed to be exact. Just re-living old times. Used to live here, you see, up at Devon House."

"What, Bovey?" she became excited, "that's where I live!"

"What a coincidence," the geese were now safely back inside the garden at the rear of the café, "would you like to meet me for a drink tonight?" he heard himself saying. She screwed up her eyes, pursed her lips and looked him straight in the face:

"At the Hotel?"

"Um…wherever…if you come at 8 we could have a meal."

"Okay…yes…that would be nice," she turned to go, "I'm Layla, by the way," and held out her hand. He took it, shook it:

"Christopher."

"Tonight then…at 8."

Walking up to the road he saw the minibus coming his way and hailed it. Sitting in the back seat, bouncing over the cattle grids, he reflected on what had been a perfect day.

30b

❀ ❀

The next day he caught the early bus to Lustleigh—a small village three miles away on the fringe of the moor. Here began one of his favourite walks—Lustleigh Cleave, the Bovey and Becka valleys, Becka Falls. He should have felt full of the joy and anticipation of the open road but the memory of his dream hung around him like an overcoat. He felt oppressed, haunted by a sense of doom. Kitty Jay, the suicide buried at the crossroads near Hound Tor had, indeed, according to legend, hung herself at a nearby farm. He knew the story well but at no time during his dream did he sense that he was participating in a latter-day re-enactment. There was a pain above and between his eyes—a tension accumulated during the night and stubbornly refusing to disperse. His stomach rumbled, reminding him that he had skipped breakfast at the hotel in order to catch the bus. The teashop in the village square probably wouldn't be open yet. Then he remembered Katherine.

Katherine was a novelist, a widow in her early forties who lived in a cottage by the Post Office. They had met, many years previously, on the Cleave. She had been meditating in the sunshine at Sharpitor, sitting cross-legged on the grass. Christopher had been standing nearby, admiring the spectacular view across the valley, when she opened her eyes. They were soon striding along the ridge towards Hunter's Tor, talking. She had taken him back to her cottage and introduced him to her husband—already ailing, it seemed—pale and walking with a stick. She wrote and said he had died a few months later but never specified the nature of his illness.

The bus dropped him at the edge of the village before turning round and heading back toward the main road. He trudged in the direction of the church and stood for a while under its lychgate. In his depression he found himself wondering how many coffins had sheltered there awaiting the arrival of the Minister. The tea-shop was, to his surprise, already open but he turned instead down a side street to where a picturesque thatched cottage stood, in its own grounds, behind a four-foot high granite wall. The gate was broken and propped against a tree-trunk.

As he entered the garden, the first drops of rain fell and his spirits sank even lower. The house looked deserted and when he knocked on the door there was no reply. He knocked again then shrugged and retraced his steps.

31b

❀ ❀

Feeling depressed, he returned to the village to buy a bottle of water and some paracetamol from the store. His head pounded as he washed two tablets down with the water. He sat slumped on a bench outside the church, waiting for them to take effect. Katherine passed him on a bicycle and he watched her disappear down the lane. Somehow he couldn't be bothered to get up and follow her.

Eventually he rose and headed off past the Cleave Hotel towards Hammerslake. The rain, which had abated awhile, now came back in earnest. Not wearing hiking boots he slipped on the stile and landed in a heap. Cursing, brushing himself off, he trudged on, head down.

A dank mist had spread out over the valleys when he reached Sharpitor. Without waiting, he descended into it. Lost in his own thoughts, he took no heed of his surroundings. Hardly pausing at the bridge, he hurled himself up the slope, hunched against the rain which soaked into his clothes. Why had he come? What was he doing here in this hostile landscape?

When he reached the café at Becka Falls, he sat sullenly in a corner and ordered coffee, scarcely noticing the striking red-haired woman who served him.

Finishing his drink, he reached the road just in time to see the minibus to Bovey Tracey disappear around a corner. Cursing his luck, he steeled himself to walk all the way back to his hotel.

32

❀ ❀

The next morning he rose early, around seven o'clock, paid his bill, and stole through the town. He passed no-one as he made his way along Fore Street, past the fire station, and onto East Street. The parish church loomed on his left. This, he remembered, was supposed to have been rebuilt by one of the de Tracey family as penance for his part in the murder of Thomas Becket in 1170 although, of what stood now, the tower dates from the fourteenth century and the remainder from the fifteenth.

Outside, the pavement rose high above the road for a short while before descending to join it again. At the bottom, through a waist-high iron gate to his left, a public footpath skirted around the back of some houses. After about fifty yards it turned and started to climb steeply. Hedgerows closed in on either side and grew together to form a canopy. He pushed on in the gloom to where some steps curved upwards until finally the path opened onto the grounds of a large house. He stopped to catch his breath and look. Just the same as it was then—a rambling granite building constructed by the church in Victorian times for 'fallen women', subsequently converted into flats, the grounds still maintained by a gardener.

His gaze scanned along the roof of the central section of the building, to where his flat had been, up six flights of stairs, right at the top. He was going to bring her here—Nancy. But it never happened.

His shoes crunched on the gravel as he skirted the grounds with its massive fir trees and circular lawn. The heavy latch on the door echoed up the stairwell, his shoes noisy on the wooden steps. Part way up he heard the door of his old flat open and a young woman with bright red hair, and a piece of toast trapped between her lips, pushed past him and clattered down the stairs.

He stared after her, open-mouthed, thinking he had seen her somewhere before, in a dream, perhaps, or maybe...

33

❀ ❀

Returning to Tapshed, he found a policeman standing outside his flat.

"Mr Purbright?"

"Yes"

"Ah…good…D.S. Harris wants a word."

"Oh?"

"Can we go inside?"

"Of course."

He inserted the key and pushed the door open.

"May I use your telephone, sir?"

"Well, I suppose so…as long as it's not long-distance."

"No sir…just HQ"

Christopher went into the kitchen and fiddled nervously with some cups and plates.

"He's here, sir," he heard the PC say, "I don't know. Do you want to speak with him? MR PURBRIGHT…D.S. HARRIS WANTS A WORD (he lowered his voice as Christopher came into the room) if you don't mind."

"Oh?"

"Mr Purbright! I distinctly asked you to stay in touch. Where have you been these last two days?"

"Up on the Moors, Superintendent. Nothing sinister. Just needed some space. Any developments?"

"None…but I must insist you keep me informed of your whereabouts."

"Yes, of course…I understand. Does this still mean that I am a suspect?"

"Mr Purbright…everyone is under suspicion…so please make my job a lot easier and keep us informed when you feel like going on another little jaunt."

"Will do. Is that all?"

"For now, sir, for now."

In his mind he could see the gold tooth glinting and the eyes squinting. He felt uneasy even though he knew this had all been staged to produce that very effect.

Part Two

'...I, always I...one always starts with I...
and ends with I.'

B. S. Johnson: *Trawl.*

34

❀ ❀

It was already 6.30...he felt tired and hungry. Heading along the Strand towards town, he filtered right, up and over Mamouth Hill, descending towards the South Western Inn. The landlord, grey hair tied back, greeted him from the bar but got his name wrong, as usual. He ordered a gammon steak and a glass of Sauvignon Blanc.

The barmaid spotted him as he slouched in the corner of the eating area, staring intently into his wineglass.

"Christopher...loved the novel. Great idea to set it around here. Really upset some people...I can tell you! No sex, thank-you, and certainly not in our back yard!" she mimicked.

He smiled:

"I know. Some hack on one of the local rags got it banned by *Smiths*. Backfired on them though— *Waterstone's* sold out and ordered more...thanks to all the fuss!"

"Really? I didn't know that. Listen...I've got my copy at home—will you sign it for me?"

"Sure."

"It's just a five-minute walk. You're not going anywhere, are you?" she gestured towards the kitchen, "I'd better ask him first, though."

"I should think so."

A few minutes later, the landlord appeared with his food.

"What have you done with my barmaid, Mark?"

"Christopher."

He stared at Christopher, a puzzled expression on his face:

"Yeah...whoever!"

35

He is walking inside a shiny corrugated iron tunnel. Nancy follows. High winds have buckled the passageway and made gaping holes in the walls, irregular twists and turns, false corridors ending in blank walls of rusted iron.

Such is the confusion of tangled metal that he takes a wrong turning which leads to a dead end. But there is a hole in the wall nearby. Pushing his head and arms through, he makes a space big enough to clamber out and finds himself half way down a wooded cliff-face. Below, the sea, blue, cool and inviting. Children are playing on the beach. He climbs a promontory with surprising ease and stands enjoying the view. Turning to help Nancy he sees that she also climbs effortlessly. But then, as she stands beside him, he sees it is no longer Nancy...it is Sarah.

❀ ❀

36

He awoke and thought of Nancy. It was late…past ten o'clock.

He went downstairs and rang the number Harris had given him.

"Hello," it was Nancy's voice.

"Nancy?"

"Chris?"

"Yes," long embarrassed pause.

"Sorry about the other day. I had to go out."

"Yeah…sorry I couldn't wait."

"Okay…it's just that Tash said you disappeared all of a sudden…without saying goodbye or anything."

"Yeah…I know…apologise to her for me. I…I…" he ran out of steam.

"Chris…"

"Nancy…we have to meet…talk about this"

"Yes…yes…I'm sorry Chris, I really am…"

"Don't…just don't…"

"When and where?"

"Tonight?"

"Can't, sorry Chris…there's so much going on here. What about Friday…I could come down to Tapshed?"

"Okay…Denby's…at eight?"

"I'll be there…bye Chris."

"Bye."

37

❀ ❀

It was Friday and he stood at the top of the churchyard steps, enjoying the view. To his left he could see the window of Ollershaw's studio. The blind was drawn.

It was late afternoon. He stood and allowed his senses to expand. Once again he felt the flow of energy from the earth, the tingling in his legs and arms. His hearing and sense of smell became more acute and his eyesight seemed to improve—he noticed details in the landscape that he had not registered before. The now familiar feeling of exhilaration returned with such force that he had to reach out and hold the metal railings at the top of the steps for support. They were cold to the touch but seemed to vibrate as if an electric current was running through them. Straightening his back, he took a deep breath and gazed out over the estuary feeling literally on top of the world. That favourite painting by Caspar David Friedrich came to mind again and in that moment Christopher knew exactly what the artist was trying to convey.

Then his stomach rumbled reminding him that he had skipped lunch. Taking the footpath that skirted the churchyard, he found himself in the cobbled alleyway outside of Ollershaw's studio. The door was slightly ajar. He knocked with his bare knuckles and called Ollershaw's name. There was a scuffling sound but no one answered. Tentatively he poked his head inside. The inner door leading from the entry to the studio was also ajar. He walked through, once more calling Ollershaw's name. Several drawers from a line of filing cabinets had been left open and some of the contents had spilled onto the floor. As he bent over to inspect some of the photographs of naked and semi-naked girls there was a flurry of activity behind him culminating in the inner and then the outer doors being slammed shut. Clearly someone had been hiding behind the studio door waiting for him to enter the room before making good his escape. Christopher sprang to the door and was just in time to see the figure of a woman with long brown hair, wearing tight blue jeans and a denim jacket, turning into Fore Street at the end of the alleyway to his right. Her face, in profile, was vaguely familiar. He shrugged and returned to the studio.

He was kneeling down examining one of the open files when Ollershaw burst in, clearly displeased:

"My God! What the hell?...What the bloody hell do you think you're doing?"

"Oh...look, I'm sorry Harry...but with the front door being open..."

"And what the bloody hell?...you've got a nerve...what are you doing with those files? I'll have the bloody police on you!"

"Look, calm down, Harry, for God's sake..."

"Calm down! Calm bloody down! How dare you!"

He lifted his fist, threatening to strike the intruder but Christopher backed-off and sat down in a nearby armchair. This gave him the breathing space he needed and took some of the wind out of Ollershaw's sails. Abruptly, Christopher stood up again:

"The police!" he shouted, "that's it! Penelope Shaw!"

Ollershaw put his hands on his hips and glared at Christopher as if he were a lunatic :

"What the bloody hell are you going on about?"

114

Christopher sat down again:

"Listen, it wasn't me who did this," he gestured at the mess on the floor, "I was trying to tell you, the front door was open and, thinking you were in, I came through. But there was somebody here, obviously going through the files, and I disturbed her. She must have hid behind that door until I was distracted and then made a dash for it. Only I caught a glimpse of her as she turned the corner and I'm fairly sure it was a woman I know called Penelope Shaw; a policewoman, in fact. She was in plain clothes—that's why I couldn't place her straight away."

Ollershaw glared at him but as Christopher's words began to sink in he turned a deathly white and for a moment it looked as if he was going to faint. Recovering, he said:

"A policewoman...in here? My God!"

With that he bounded to the far end of the studio, threw aside an easy chair to expose a safe set into the wall, fiddled with the lock, cursing all the while, finally opened it and breathed a plainly audible sigh of relief:

"Bloody hell!"

Shutting the safe, he collapsed into a chair then looked across to where Christopher was sitting:

"What did you say her name was?"

"Shaw...Penelope Shaw...I'm almost sure."

Ollershaw jumped to his feet and started rifling through the open filing cabinet:

"Was she carrying anything?"

"I couldn't really say...sorry. Look, what is all this? Why should an ordinary policewoman in plain clothes be going through your files?"

But Ollershaw was not listening. He had crossed the room to a desk and was flipping through a card index:

"Shaw...Shaw?...SHAW! Penelope Shaw—so that's it!" he waved a card at Christopher, "policewoman, you say?"

Christopher nodded.

Ollershaw looked up at the ceiling, squinting, trying to remember:

"Hmmm...yes...did some work for me a year or so ago...good looking girl..."

"What, modelling?" Christopher was taken by surprise.

"Yeah, don't think anything ever came of it though. But I said I'd keep her on file," he had crossed to the filing cabinet again, "her bloody file's missing."

Christopher looked puzzled:

"But that's ridiculous. Why didn't she just ask you for the file?"

Ollershaw sat down again and put a hand over his eyes:

"I don't know...unless!" he returned to the wall safe and once again fiddled with the lock until it opened. He extracted a small box containing half-a-dozen videos:

"Listen, Chris, could you do me a big favour? Will you look after these for a few days—just until I ask for them back. They're for a special customer, you see. Worth a lot of money to me, they are. But...well...I'll level with you...they're a bit strong—for someone with special tastes—and I'm afraid that if the police find them here I could be in big trouble."

Christopher looked puzzled and distinctly unsure:

"You mean Penelope Shaw was really looking for these?"

"No, I don't think so. I think she found what she was looking for. But it would seem from her actions that the police intend to pay me a visit, a surprise visit and that she caught wind of this and didn't want them to find her photographs."

"You mean a raid!"

"Sort of...well, yes, a raid...it's happened before to a friend of mine. They took away everything and went through it thoroughly. Luckily he didn't have anything too controversial on the premises."

"Good grief!"

Ollershaw pushed the box onto Christopher's lap. He looked unhappy and tried to push it away:

"Look, why me? Surely there's someone else you could entrust them with. I mean, you scarcely know me."

"There's no time and, besides, they may be watching me. Here," taking the box off him, he placed it in a carrier bag, "that'll look less conspicuous."

Before he could say anything more, the bag was in his hands and Ollershaw was escorting him to the door.

"Thanks, Mark. I really am most grateful to you. Look after these," he tapped the bag, "I'll be in touch."

It was only after the door had closed, and he was making his way along the alley, that he realised Harry had called him 'Mark' and, for some reason, this sent a shiver down his spine.

38

The sky was clouding over as he walked along High Street towards Denby's Wine Bar, promising rain in the night. But it was still warm for the time of year. The houses and shops lining each side of the road all displayed police posters in their windows bearing a rather grainy photograph of his daughter. He stopped and examined her face closely. She had all her mother's facial features: tiny button nose, high cheekbones, thin lips. The resemblance was remarkable although the eyes and head were downcast as if nothing in the world around her was of any interest. Almost as if, and this made him shudder, she was already dead when the photograph was taken. The dark half-circles under her eyes were far too pronounced for someone of her age and the hair was lank and untidy. She had, he thought, the look of a loser and, despite her age, seemed resigned to her fate.

Turning, he was startled to find someone standing next to him, peering over his shoulder—an elderly man in a raincoat.

"Terrible thing," he muttered, shaking his head.

"Hmmm…I wonder what's happened to her?"

The old man shook his head again, pursing his lips:

"Oh…she's dead," he mumbled, "almost certainly."

39

❀ ❀

Denby's was already comfortably full as he squeezed through the tiny double doors but a quick circuit of the rooms revealed that Nancy had not yet arrived. Luckily a young couple was just vacating the tiny table for two tucked just inside the entrance. He put his coat on one of the chairs and took the empty glasses to the bar, ordering a bottle of Chablis and two glasses. Taking them back to his table he sat and gazed around the room. He found himself listening to the conversation of the three people—two women and a man—sitting around the table next to him who were obviously expecting two others to join their party to fill the empty seats where their coats were piled. They were all, he thought, in their mid-thirties; a blonde woman: slim, attractive and very self-assured; a brunette, who they called Jean, equally attractive with full sensual lips but slightly nervous and restrained. The man had a neatly trimmed black beard which made him look older than his years, his voice deep, speech measured and intelligent.

The doors opened and, to his discomfort, in came Alison looking absolutely stunning in a thin white knee-length coat and canvas shoes. Her face was noticeably but not overpoweringly made-up and her hair pinned back in a seemingly hurried fashion with strands hanging here and there which could easily have been carefully contrived to give the impression of having just stepped out of bed. But it was the man who followed her in that had the greater effect on Christopher. For the second time that evening he shuddered...but he couldn't think why. Certainly he had never, to his knowledge, seen this man before...and yet...?

Alison walked past him—if she noticed his presence she gave no sign. Both women instinctively surveyed her from head to toe, their critical faculties working overtime. There was a certain amount of tension in the air.

"Alison, I'd like you to meet my wife Helen and our friends Jean and Adrian."

They all smiled sheepishly and shuffled uneasily in their seats. Alison, clearly taken-aback, quickly recovered, flashed her companion what appeared to Christopher, even from a distance, as an 'I'll get even with you, you bastard' look, then smiled, nodded to each in turn and removed her coat. Underneath she was wearing a tight yellow tee-shirt and obviously nothing underneath. Adrian did his best to look nonchalant as she slid onto the seat next to him but was obviously unsettled by her close proximity. Her companion, Helen's husband, sat between her and Helen, opposite Jean who was concentrating over-hard, he thought, on pouring them two glasses of wine. She had a puzzled look on her face as if struggling in her mind to make sense of the situation.

"How are you?" she asked Helen's husband.

"Fine...and you?"

"Oh...fine."

Leaning forward, she set a glass of wine in front of him, then pushed the other towards Alison. To hide her discomfort she arched her back, brought her hands up behind her neck and splayed her long, wavy black hair out over each shoulder.

"So you're Alison," he heard Helen saying, "I've been looking forward to meeting you."

Alison glanced at her fleetingly over the rim of her glass then, taking a long draught, completely emptied it and reached for the bottle to pour another:

"I'm glad to meet you too," she said, keeping her eyes firmly fixed on the wine glass, "I've heard a lot about you, of course. You work for a publishing company don't you?"

"Hmm, yes, John Crape."

Alison stifled a snigger. Helen gave her husband a long-suffering glance and added something Christopher didn't quite catch.

"Such as?" was his response.

Averting her eyes she gazed up and into one of the spotlights in a corner of the ceiling:

"Let's not go into that now, shall we. What do you do Alison? Oh, I forgot, you're a student aren't you. How are your studies progressing?"

"Well, I'm only a first-year but we do have some important exams at the end of the month so I'm working pretty hard at the moment. Mark has been very helpful, as you probably know."

'Mark!...*his* name is Mark,' thought Christopher and then wondered why he had considered that to be so important.

Helen smiled, shot a glance at Mark, raised her eyebrows but refrained from any further comment. There was an uneasy silence. Adrian got to his feet:

"Another bottle?" he asked.

At this point Nancy entered and slipped into the seat beside him before he had time to rise and greet her. She looked haggard and even thinner than usual. From a distance she didn't look old enough to be in a wine bar but up-close he could see the dark half-circles under her eyes and the hollows of her cheeks. When she looked down into her drink, which he had poured for her, she looked remarkably like the picture of her daughter...their daughter...which lined the streets outside.

"Nancy..." he put his hand on hers.

She started to cry and buried her head in his shoulder.

Mark called out from the bar:

"Helen, did you know about this? Adrian's landed a senior lecturer's job. Plymouth Poly."

Helen looked surprised, then pleased. Looking toward Adrian she flashed him a congratulatory grin and raised her glass:

"Adrian...tremendous news...you are a clever boy."

Puckering her lips, she blew him a kiss. Adrian grinned and looked down at his feet.

"So it's true then?" he said to Nancy when she had recovered.

"Yes...she is yours. I'm sorry Chris...I...and now she's gone...I don't know what to do..." she started crying again then broke away, blew her nose and finished her wine, like Alison, in one draught.

"I need something stronger..." she walked over to the bar and returned with a double vodka.

"Have you no idea where she might be?" he asked.

She looked at him and didn't answer. It was a stupid question.

"We thought that maybe you..."

"Nancy...I had no idea. And anyway, kidnapping is not my scene, especially not a kid. I wouldn't know what to do with her."

"Yeah...yeah...it was a long shot. We were desperate

we ARE desperate! The police…well…they're doing their best."

Christopher finished the wine and bought another bottle. The conversation was getting animated on the table next to them.

Helen leaned forward against the table, knocking over an empty glass, and stared at Jean from close quarters, hoping to note her reactions in detail:

"Alison screws my husband," she said drunkenly, "he screws her while I'm in London screwing somebody else's husband."

Mouths fell open; Adrian choked on his drink; several people standing nearby stopped their various conversations and turned momentarily in their direction then away again to return half-heartedly to what they were saying, ears cocked for any other juicy snippets. Alison distracted herself by thumping Adrian on the back. Jean looked down at her hands which were firmly pushed into her lap. Helen giggled wickedly, delighted at the reaction:

"Don't worry Jean, my dear, the relationship has my blessing. I think it's a good thing for a husband and wife to have affairs, as long as they're careful. It makes life interesting. After all, I can't really expect him to be faithful. Sexually active people like Mark here need regular sex, don't you darling?" she patted his hand.

He glared at her through a semi-drunken haze and a cloud of cigarette smoke, unable to say a word. All ears in the small front room of the wine bar were now firmly tuned-in and there was a certain amount of smirking and nudging and giggling going on. Helen continued, in an even louder voice, aware of her rapt audience:

"So, you see, we pursue our own sex lives during the

week then come together (so to speak) every other weekend to compare notes. It's a great turn-on—you should try it Jean. By rights, I should be in London this weekend, hence the presence of young Alison here. And you two turning up has really confused things, I can tell you."

Alison flashed her a look of unadulterated malice:

"I think I should be going," she said, rising shakily to her feet. Mark recovered sufficiently to restrain her:

"No, not at all. You've missed your last train anyway. You'll stay the night. You too," he nodded at Jean and Adrian, "you're too drunk to drive anywhere. You can have the spare bedroom."

Adrian nodded his thanks. Alison resumed her seat and glared into her half empty glass. Helen had buried her face in her arms and was slouched forward onto the table. Suddenly she looked up and erupted into peals of uncontrollable laughter, laughter so infectious that within seconds, despite themselves, the whole company—even Alison—found irresistible. Christopher and Nancy looked at each other and shook their heads in disbelief.

"Come on. Let's get out of here. These people think they've got problems. They don't know the half of it."

He gulped down the wine in his glass but left the bottle half full. As he walked to the door he could feel Mark's eyes following him but when he turned to let Nancy through, he saw that, in fact, he had his back to him.

40

❀ ❀

They staggered out of Denby's and turned right towards the town centre. But their progress was unsteady and slow, stopping often, and when they reached the church he led her to one side:

"Come on, let's go and listen to the mud."

She stifled a laugh:

"Mud? Sounds romantic."

"Not so much romantic, more...contemplative, restful even. Help us think things through."

They turned right, past the bookshop and through the churchyard. A cool breeze, blowing across the estuary from the west, carrying the occasional droplet of rain, freshened their faces. Instinctively they breathed deeply revelling in the feeling of exhilaration it produced. Nancy tossed back her head, allowing her hair to stream out behind her. They stood awhile at the top of the churchyard steps experiencing the view. There was no one else around. Across the river and canal, beyond the marshes, the lights of Exminster stood out clear and bright. A train to Plymouth and Cornwall snaked its way along—the sound of its progress filtering across the water loud and clear although easily a mile distant. To the north, car headlights could be seen on the motorway bridge. A giant orange halo hung over the city of Exeter.

A light came on in Ollershaw's studio but this went unnoticed by Christopher who was looking the other way.

The tide was partially out and as they descended the concrete steps the sound of the train gave way to the steady trickle, trickle, trickling of the water as it filtered through the mud. It was a slightly eerie noise which, paradoxically, he found infinitely comforting. Hearing it instantly transported him back to the days of his youth. As a teenager he had spent whole evenings sitting in the dark listening to this sound, thinking. The sense of being physically transported back in time was so strong that for a moment he completely lost contact with the here and now and actually became the confused young boy struggling to make sense of his life. Then, as he regained his senses, he experienced a terrible feeling of claustrophobia as the clutter of twenty years reformed itself around him, layer upon layer, like an onion. Nancy had broken away from him and was walking down the causeway, still with her head held high and hair streaming, enjoying the breeze. He sat down on one of the benches and covered his face with his hands. It had come as a profound shock to him. In just those few moments he had seen quite clearly that he had lost his direction and that, if anything, the confused teenager was more of a complete person than the mature man. Somehow, all the lofty ideals, all the dreams of fulfilment, all the excitement and challenge of the Quest had dissipated and he was left with a profound feeling of nostalgia and melancholy. Desperately he wanted, needed, to return, to empty himself and start again. He trembled with emotion and the tears, falling onto his hands, filtered between his fingers. Nancy was walking back towards him and he did not wish her to see him like this. Pulling a handkerchief from his pocket, he blew his nose and quickly dabbed at his eyes.

He smiled up at her as she came near and sat down next to him. He felt fresher and clearer as if a great burden had been shed and wiped away with the tears. She moved close to him and shuddered.

"Are you cold?" he asked, "do you want to go?"

Since leaving Denby's she had hardly spoken a word. He had sensed her need to be left in silence and had not pressed conversation on her. Now, as she looked at him, tears began to form in her eyes. He put an arm around her shoulder:

"I've lost my way," she said, almost inaudibly, "I need help."

He stared at her in disbelief then laughed hollowly and shook his head:

"I'm in no position to help you, Nancy. You see, I was just thinking the very same thing about myself. It came to me just now...as I was sitting here. I suddenly remembered how I was as a teenager. And it seemed to me that between then and now I'd somehow lost track of what I was searching for. I admit that I didn't really know exactly what I was after even then but, you know, life was there for the taking, the gauntlet had been thrown down and I was at least thinking about stooping to pick it up. For a time I may have even held it in my hands, or put it on and waved it about but now, suddenly, when I look, it's not there anymore. I seem to have dropped it somewhere or, more likely, it's slipped off my hand at some stage and the only way I can retrieve it is by retracing my steps."

She buried her head in his shoulder and they stayed like that for several minutes. He made no attempt to comfort her with words, knowing that she would feel better after having cried it out of her system. When she finally lifted her head from his shoulder he instinctively kissed her gently on the forehead. She smiled, said goodbye and walked away from him. All at once he felt drained and ready for sleep; his legs would barely support him. But his mind remained clear and alert. He called her name but she did not turn...just continued walking until she disappeared as the road curved. He sat down again and stared out across the river without really looking. When he felt able to stand, he headed off in the opposite direction. As he walked beneath Ollershaw's studio the light from the window flashed light and shadow, light and shadow, as if someone had knocked the shade and sent it swinging. Christopher stopped under a streetlamp and looked down. Something lay on the ground at his feet. Bending over, he picked up a nearly new leather glove:

'Another gauntlet...' he thought, laughing out loud, '...with a button at the wrist. Perhaps this one won't slip off so easily.'

As he held it up, the light in Ollershaw's studio went out.

❀ ❀

41

❀ ❀

He poured himself a glass of wine and brought the bottle through to the living room. Without turning on the light he went to the window. His foot kicked against the bag of videos. Swearing loudly he set the wine on the sill and, retracing his steps, switched on the light. Picking up the bag, he peered inside. The tapes had been hastily bound together with sellotape. He broke the tape with his nail and removed the uppermost, which he placed into the video recorder. Collecting his wine, he sat on Tarkovsky and watched.

After a few seconds of flashing numbers the title "ALICE IN FUNDERLAND" appeared on the screen. He chuckled as a muscular man, naked, with a huge erection sauntered across a room and arranged himself on some cushions. He was joined soon afterwards by another man of similar build but with more body hair. They looked bored and began to idly stroke themselves. Soon a well-developed girl, dressed only in stockings, suspender-belt and red high-heeled shoes, came into shot, joined the men on the cushions and the action commenced culminating ten minutes later with both men ejaculating simul-taneously over the her face.

Meanwhile the camera slowly panned back to show that all this activity was taking place for the benefit of the members of some exclusive club, which Christopher recognised as the Riverwalk, who somehow managed to sit quietly in the semi-darkness, sipping cocktails. Red velvet curtains finally fell across the stage as the three performers lay in a huddle on the cushions. There was a ripple of applause drowned almost immediately by the sound of pop music with a disco beat. Nancy, dressed in tennis skirt, white tee-shirt and plimsolls, carrying a racket, was spotlighted among the audience. She began dancing among the tables, stopping every now and then to bend over and rub the handle of the racket between her legs. The camera retreated steadily until it became apparent that the filming was taking place from an adjacent room through a one-way mirror. Leaning against the mirror, looking out into the auditorium and stage, was a young girl with blonde hair that flowed down to her waist. A door was opened behind her flooding the room with light. She turned and a shadow fell across her naked underdeveloped body. Her hand went instinctively to the side of her face, pushing the hair behind one ear, as she contrived a welcoming smile. This too was Nancy, by some trick in the editing.

A cultured man's voice was heard:

"Alice. I'd like you to meet Mr. Smith. You'll take good care of him for me, won't you?"

She smiled again:

"Yes, Daddy, I'll do whatever Mr. Smith says."

"Good girl. I'll see you later Mr. Smith."

The room resumed its semi-darkness as the door was closed. The girl turned toward the auditorium where the tennis player, having removed her tee-shirt to reveal small firm breasts, was inviting a male member of the audience to suck one of her nipples.

"That's my mummy out there, Mr. Smith. Do you like her?"

A large shadowy figure came into shot and stood next to the girl with his back to the camera. He laid a hand on her shoulder and allowed it to stray slowly down her back and across her buttocks.

"Hmmm," came the almost breathless reply, "but I like you better. Why don't you come and sit on my knee."

Christopher turned it off. He couldn't bear to watch anymore. It brought back too many memories. Rewinding the tape and replacing it in its jacket, he took his glass and bottle of wine to bed. He had drunk too much but wished to drink more. When the bottle was empty, he switched off the light, lay back and relaxed. The room spun. Rain pattered against the window. He breathed-in deeply then exhaled and experienced an acute feeling of bliss. Again he was transported, momentarily, back to his youth. He was in the attic at Mamouth Street, which he had painted black and adorned with all manner of mystical symbols and charms, listening as the elements lulled him off to sleep.

42

❀ ❀

Even though Christopher was exhausted, he slept badly. His mind raced uncontrollably, recycling thoughts and throwing up unpleasant images. When the morning sunlight, squeezing through a gap in the curtains, fell directly on his face, he awoke feeling as if he had not slept at all. There was a dull ache above his eyes and thoughts came to him as if filtered through a thick wad of cotton wool. It was as though he were sitting huddled somewhere in the back of his head unwilling to come forward and take on the responsibility of controlling his mind. His throat was dry, his body ached and he felt like retreating even further into his mind or, better still, moving outside of his body altogether whilst it went about the process of healing itself. Was this what death was like—a gradual retreat from a body too old or too sick to be worth the effort of retaining? In that case death seemed to be a voluntary affair, an almost conscious resignation. Or perhaps the reverse was true—maybe the body and the mind conspire to push you out. After all, most people do not wish to die and some die violent and hasty deaths. No, there was no doubt in his mind that the body and mind were machines incapable of working without a controller. So no matter how hasty or violent, the quitting of the mind and body at death has to be an individual decision, a choice for the better. A new life in a new body, perhaps?

He needed a cup of coffee and slowly groped his way to the kitchen. There was a note lying on the doormat.

His Christian name was scrawled on the front. It was from Ollershaw:

MEET ME AT GOAT WALK, MIDNIGHT MONDAY. BRING TAPES. MUCH APPRECIATE YOUR HELP. H.O.

He smirked thinking it all a bit over-dramatic. Almost as if Harry had been watching too many detective films.

Making some coffee, he took it back upstairs and gulped the contents thankfully. Never, he thought, had a cup of coffee tasted better. He put the mug on the floor then propped himself with pillows against the wall. Closing his eyes, he surrendered himself to the calming effect of the drink. He breathed deeply at first, feeling the cool air rushing up his nose and down into his lungs. Gradually, as his breathing became more and more shallow, he started to systematically relax his body starting from the toes and working up to his brow. This worked to a certain extent but did not entirely dispel the pressure in his head. The turmoil of the night's events had created a knot of tension that could only be successfully unravelled by a personal confrontation with Harry himself.

The boat
❀ ❀

The sun was rising, slowly dispelling the mist that hung over the Exe Estuary. The water was so still and calm that it looked solid. He sat on the footpath, known locally as the Goat Walk, dangling his feet over the wall. The tide was in and the water reached to within a few inches of the soles of his shoes. This was another favourite haunt of his youth—particularly beautiful at sunset when the sun disappeared behind Haldon Hills and Dartmoor, staining the clouds yellow then orange, sometimes red then pink, reflecting them in the water. The Goat Walk itself was a curious construction—a twelve-foot stone wall around a field at the end of the Strand, staggered halfway by a five-foot wide concrete pathway along which benches had been fixed at intervals. When the tide was out it was possible to walk and even drive a car on the muddy stone bed of the river below the pathway, thus connecting the Strand and Bowling Green Road, both of which ended in slipways.

He closed his eyes and listened to the silence broken occasionally by the melancholy cries of the wildfowl in the sanctuary across the river. Suddenly, without opening his eyes, he saw his legs and feet and the surface of the river and he felt, with all certainty, that if he was to stand-up and push himself forward he could walk upon the water without any form of support. It seemed as if his body had shed all its substance and that he was floating slightly above it held by the slenderest of silken threads. He'd experienced this kind of weightlessness before, in dreams, where he had been able to hover above the ground or pass through solid walls. But this was no dream. Slowly he lowered himself from the wall. Then, as if by magic, the mist parted and he saw, way out in the navigation channel, a large cabin cruiser. On deck he saw the small figure of a young girl waving at him and calling his name. The sudden shock brought him back into himself and he once again felt the heaviness of his body, became gripped with fear and somehow just managed to push himself back onto the walkway before he fell into the water.

A small dingy was tied-up at the Strand end of the Walk. He ran toward it, jumped aboard and cast-off. There were no paddles. He steadied the boat, aimed it in the right direction and pushed-off from the wall. The dingy went steadily in the required direction and it was small and light enough for him to be able to 'paddle' using both hands. The mist closed around him again and he lost sight of both the boat and the shore. He stopped paddling and peered into the dense white wall trying to make out the outline of the boat. A few seconds later it loomed up in front of him and he hauled himself on board. Securing the dingy to the side rail he quickly surveyed the deck. It was deserted. Tentatively he pushed at the cabin doors which opened inwards to reveal the sleeping and cooking quarters. This too appeared deserted. He sat down to think. Was he on the wrong boat? No, impossible...boats were not allowed to moor this far down river. There was a sudden noise on deck and someone slammed the cabin doors shut. He jumped forward and pulled at them but found them locked:

"Who's out there?" he shouted, hammering on the door, "who's out there?"

His voice was drowned by the engine starting up and the boat began to move steadily down the estuary. Shaking his head in disbelief he sat down again and looked around him. There was a blue plastic skylight immediately above him. He pushed at it but that too was securely fastened. Looking around again he saw a door to the left of the barred entrance—obviously a store cupboard or W.C.. He pulled at the handle. The door opened toward him and the naked body of a young girl, jammed inside, fell forward and knocked him over. At that instant the cabin doors burst open and there with the mist swirling around him, stood Detective Superintendent Harris.

Christopher sat bolt upright in bed. It was still dark and the rain was now hammering against the window.

Wide awake now, he slipped out of bed and groped his way downstairs. His mouth and throat were desperately dry and his head still swam from the excess of wine. He reached the living room and with trembling hands took the video from its jacket and inserted it into the machine, fast-forwarding to the place where he had switched off:

"...why don't you come and sit on my knee."

The girl turned toward the camera, her face still partially shrouded in shadow. With a pounding heart he watched as the girl padded across the floor. Fleetingly her features were illuminated by a spotlight bulb in the ceiling. He stopped the film, rewound it slightly, and then froze the frame at the appropriate moment. Supposing that *wasn't* Nancy...supposing it was Alison, his daughter, swathed in a long wig of blonde hair. That would explain why Harry wanted to offload the tapes. As he switched off the recorder he felt his stomach tighten. Perspiration glistened on his brow and his heart felt as if it would explode. He staggered into the kitchen and vomited into the sink. A cool fresh wave of relief swept over him as he turned his back to the sink and slid slowly to the floor. He began to shake violently. Pulling himself to his feet he turned the cold tap on full, washed his face and gargled the bad taste from his mouth and throat. He then went back to the sitting room, re-wound the tape, put it in the bag and went upstairs to bed.

He was going to have to pay another visit to Harry.

44

❀ ❀

It was a pleasant afternoon as Christopher made his way along the Strand towards Ollershaw's studio.

The sun, shining up the street, was warm and pleasing, heralding the long-awaited summer months. He felt safe and secure as if starting a new life. A couple of paracetamol had taken the edge off his headache and he relaxed completely, breathing in the warming air.

He had reached the point on Fore Street where the cobbled alleyway, that led to Ollershaw's studio, branched off. There his progress was arrested by two police cars blocking the entrance. Naturally curious, he weaved between the empty cars and into the alleyway. At that very instant Detective Superintendent Harris stepped out of Ollershaw's doorway and walked briskly toward him. Christopher flinched, remembering his dream. Faltering for an instant he panicked, almost turning on his heels and fleeing as fast as his legs would carry him. But Harris had obviously spotted and recognised him. So he suppressed the panic and walked on:

"Good afternoon, Superintendent!" he announced, deliberately drawing attention to himself.

"Ah...good afternoon, sir," the thick lips smiled a professional rather than a spontaneous smile, the eyes squinted, the gold tooth glinted, "coming to see our friend Mr. Ollershaw are we."

It was more of a statement than a question.

"Why...uh...no. As a matter of fact I was just on my way to enjoy the view across the river."

Christopher looked toward the open doorway where a hefty police constable now stood:

"What's going on?"

Harris smirked:

"You wouldn't happen to know the whereabouts of Mr. Ollershaw would you?"

"Why...no...no, I wouldn't. To tell you the truth I don't know very much about him at all. Is he in some kind of trouble?"

Again Harris ignored his enquiry. Widening his eyes in mock surprise he said:

"Really sir? I heard that you and he were quite good friends."

Christopher began to feel distinctly uncomfortable but shrugged and tried to sound convincing:

"Well really, Superintendent. I don't know who told you that but it's not strictly true. We have met occasionally. But really, I hardly know the man...except to say that he's some sort of a photographer."

"Some sort, sir?"

"Well...um...glamour, I believe," Christopher shuffled with embarrassment and looked down at his feet.

"Hmmm...indeed," Harris nodded toward the door, "have you ever been in there?"

Christopher panicked again, then heard himself replying:

"Why, yes, but only once or twice. Yesterday afternoon, in fact."

Harris's eyes fixed upon his and squinted even more than usual as if he was trying to see right into his brain:

"Oh yes?"

"Yes...I...I was just passing and I saw his door open. So I decided to say hello."

"But I thought you said you hardly knew him?"

"That's right..." all at once Christopher's brain cleared and he saw the need to change the direction of the conversation, "look, Superintendent—what is this all about?"

"Well sir, it seems Mr.Ollershaw has had his place done over, so to speak...by person or persons unknown...as yet."

"Oh!" Christopher's mouth fell open and he struggled in vain for words.

"Yes, a right old mess! Neighbour called us early this morning. Door was open and some bits and pieces scattered along the alley here. Any thoughts on who might want to do such a thing?"

"No, none whatsoever. As I said, I scarcely know the man. Anyway, forgive me for asking, but I wouldn't have thought that a simple housebreaking would be of interest to you."

"Hmmm, not normally sir. But as it is, everything that happens in this town is of interest to me; until, that is, we've found Alison Moltby and...um...cleared up any associated matters."

Christopher's mind was again in turmoil. Should he come clean and tell Harris about the videos? He still couldn't believe that Ollershaw was in any way connected with Alison's disappearance or possible murder. Clearly he would have destroyed the videos if that was so. Revealing their existence to Harris would only get him into unnecessary trouble. He decided against...until he had talked to Ollershaw personally and extracted some sort of explanation from him.

"Was there much damage done to the flat?" he asked, "he has some valuable equipment in there. I suppose that was what they were after?"

Harris about-turned and took him by the arm:

"See for yourself, sir."

Christopher gasped as they stepped inside the studio. It looked as if a raging bull had been set loose inside it. Files and photographs littered the floor, furniture had been overturned and much of the equipment smashed:

"My God!" was all he could find to say. Harris restrained him from stepping into the room where two men in overalls were sitting through the wreckage:

"No further if you don't mind, sir. We don't want this disturbed until we've gone through it carefully."

Christopher recoiled:

"Yes...yes, of course."

He glanced along the wall to where the safe had been. Harris followed his gaze:

"Made off with the safe, it seems," he said nonchalantly.

Christopher tried to sound surprised:

"Safe?"

"Hmmm...that hole in the wall down there. Obviously contained a safe of some kind. Ripped clean out of the wall. Any idea what he might have kept in there, sir?"

"None whatsoever...money?"

"Hmmm, perhaps," Harris sighed, took Christopher by the arm again and returned to the alleyway:

"One more question before you go, Mr. Wright..."

"Purbright," Christopher corrected him.

His eyes squinted as if in disbelief:

"Oh…yes…indeed, sir, Purbright. Now, where was I? Yes…how was Mr. Ollershaw when you saw him yesterday? Did he seem alright to you? Worried about anything; seem out of sorts; disturbed in any way ?"

"No...he seemed his usual self, as far as I could tell. I must repeat, Superintendent, I hardly know the man."

Harris sounded unconvinced:

"Hmmm, so you said, sir, so you said. Anyway, I won't detain you any longer. But I may need to question you again later," he shot Christopher a penetrating glance, "incidentally, there is some rumour going round that Mr. Ollershaw was into something a bit more, shall we say, daring, than glamour photography. Something a bit more lucrative and...well... specialised."

Christopher could feel his heart beating faster:

"You mean...pornographic?"

Harris nodded. Christopher shook his head disbelievingly:

"Oh, come now, this is Tapshed not Soho. Hardly the centre of such activities! Believe me, Superintendent, I was brought up here. Nothing like that could go on in these parts. To be honest I found it difficult to believe that Harry…um…Ollershaw was even involved in the glamour business—just doesn't look the type. But his photographs, the ones I've seen anyway, seem harmless enough and even, dare I say it, tasteful. I'm pretty certain he wouldn't be involved in anything sordid."

"Hmmm, yes, well, as you said, you didn't know him very well did you sir?"

Christopher was slightly taken aback by this turnabout:

"Yes...yes. Well, if that's all, I'll say goodbye."

"Good-day sir."

142

He could feel Harris's eyes boring into his back as he walked the rest of the alleyway. A cooling breeze played over his face as he came out into the churchyard and he suddenly realised how hot and sticky he had become during the course of what had been little short of an interrogation. Extracting a handkerchief from his trouser pocket, he wiped the perspiration from his brow.

45

✹ ✹

That evening, under the cover of darkness, a man, Christopher Purbright, for reasons known only to himself, left his home, proceeded along the Strand, in the direction of the town centre, turned right up Mamouth Hill, then right again into Mamouth Street. A cold penetrating wind caused him to turn up the collar of his coat. There were those who had said that this was the coldest street in Tapshed, but that was thirty years ago—a conversation overheard in the barber's shop as he sat waiting his turn. In those days he had not felt the cold—the sun, it seemed, had always shone—and would have disagreed with the speakers had he not been a mere boy in a room full of men. For it was here, in Tapshed, that he had been born and brought-up; down this very road he had run, time and time again, clutching a half-crown and repeating over-and-over the items his mother had sent him to purchase from the corner shop. But now, thirty years on, he seldom ran anywhere, the north wind chilled him to the bone, the corner shop was gone and the street was full of the ghosts of dead relatives and neighbours. It was indeed the coldest street in Tapshed.

He reached the house near the top, with a diamond shape cut into the plaster above the front door, and stood under the street light opposite for many minutes before crossing over, listening for any sounds from within, then tentatively pushing the handle downwards and pressing his weight against the door. A voice rang out from inside:

"Who's there?"

Startled, he scurried away across Mamouth Avenue and was lost in the darkness.

46

❀ ❀

The Alison Moltby case was front page news in the *Sunday Times* and continued inside where a full-length picture of Nancy was printed on page five. The article described her as a waitress at Exeter's Riverwalk Club, 'a notorious night-spot'. There was no mention, of course, of a father—Alison and her mother, apparently, lived alone.

Christopher, having risen early and walked to the news-agents, was seated in his chair, sipping coffee, reading avidly.

Interesting 'evidence' from a French clairvoyant, Claude Reveaux, was appended to the article. Apparently he had been useful to the French authorities in helping to locate missing persons. His method was a kind of dowsing, using a pendulum. Operating from his home in Paris, Reveaux had, first of all, held his pendulum over a photograph of the girl and declared, with great confidence, that she was still alive. He then went on to pinpoint her whereabouts by using at first a large-scale map of the Exeter area (from which he got no response) and then progressing to smaller-scale maps of Devon, the South West and finally England. Apparently he got no response from the pendulum at all until he came to the map of England and it began to swing over the East Midlands. Larger scale maps then narrowed the location down to the Nottingham area where, coincidentally, Alison had an uncle. Police, however, were unconvinced, having already ruled him out of their enquiries. The article went on to outline some of the more bizarre psychic 'help' the police had received. Christopher had always felt that there was more to life than met the eye and had read many books on mysticism and the occult but he couldn't help feeling just a little sorry for the police when faced with all this often conflicting barrage of supernatural 'evidence'.

47

❀ ❀

Christopher placed two slices of toast under the grill and grated some cheese. There was a tomato in the fridge which he cut into slices. The cheese went on the toast, the tomato went on the cheese and the slices were put back under the grill. Meanwhile he made a cup of instant coffee which he placed on a tray beside the plate of sizzling cheese on toast.

He sat part-way up the stairs and ate his lunch looking out over the river to the hills beyond.

A thought struck him and, on an impulse, he left the tray on the stairs, slipped on his coat, checking his pockets for loose-change and his wallet for something more substantial, and went out of the front door, slamming it shut behind him. It was a dull, overcast day; he huddled into his coat as he turned left onto the Strand and walked to the Quay where a minibus to Exeter was waiting in the car park by the pub. He bought a ticket from the driver and sat down. It was late afternoon. No one else was on the bus.

Half-an-hour later he was in the nearly deserted High Street shopping centre. Daffodils, set in concrete tubs on the pavements, bobbed their heads in the breeze as he passed. It was growing colder and prematurely dark. He buttoned his coat, which he had undone in the overheated bus, and pushed his hands deep into his pockets. St. Martin's Lane opened onto the wide expanse of the Cathedral Yard. The sudden view of the cathedral, in all its splendour, took his breath away and he could never resist cutting through there to gain access to South Street rather than take the more direct route through the shopping centre. He was not a religious man—not in the sense that most people would interpret the word—but the sight of that immense Gothic structure, with its twelfth century towers, always uplifted him. As he skirted round it towards the impressive West Front—where a few early tourists had gathered in a huddle on the concourse—he felt his shoulders straighten, his body relax and his senses sharpen. Probably this was due not so much to the building itself but to the site on which it was built. Perhaps it was here that powerful earth forces converged, (as at Stonehenge or Glastonbury, so it is said) profoundly affecting the unconscious mind. Whatever the cause, the effect was always beneficial.

Passing out of the Close and into South Street, he paused at the traffic lights before crossing and proceeding along Fore Street. After about fifty yards the street inclined sharply, dropping toward the River Exe. This was the part of the shopping centre that had always interested him the most. Small specialist shops, forced out of the city centre by high rents, made their homes on either side of the street. Second-hand booksellers, small restaurants, cafes, pubs, do-it-yourself, antiques, cut-price furnishing, sex aids and craft shops all rubbed shoulders. But today he walked swiftly, scarcely noticing the window displays, allowing the force of gravity to propel him onward toward his objective. Abruptly the buildings ended and before him lay the road system designed to relieve the bottleneck that existed when Exeter had only one Exe Bridge. Now there were two, one an entrance to, the other an exit from, the city.

Across the nearest bridge, on the far bank, he could see quite clearly the neon signs of a clutch of nightclubs, one of which he knew to be the 'Riverwalk'.

48

✿ ✿

The weather had taken a turn for the worse as he crossed Exe Bridge. The wind had veered round from the north and something resembling sleet had begun to fall from the sky.

As he reached the doors of the club, he was surprised to see someone who looked remarkably like the man who had escorted Alison into Denby's last night, being pushed out onto the pavement by a portly bouncer—probably in his late twenties but looking ten years older—dressed in a dark suit which he'd either grown out of or, more likely, inherited from a smaller man. The man stumbled past him and was away before Christopher could get a good look.

"An' what be you wantin', zur?" the bouncer snarled, sarcastically, in a broad Devonshire accent.

"I'd like to see Gerard, please...Gerard Anthony."

"Oh would 'e now, zur?" more sarcasm, "now, we jus' 'ad enough of you journalist-types yer fer one day. Zo clear off!"

He thrust out a huge agricultural mitt and pushed Christopher backwards. Recovering himself, he stood tall, looked the man in the eyes and said,

"Would you please tell him Christopher...Christopher Purbright is here to see him?"

"Christopher...my dear boy!" a smooth cultured voice echoed down an unlit staircase to their right. A silver chain supporting a notice marked 'PRIVATE' barred the way. Christopher peered into the gloom and just made out a tall, elegant, elderly man with silver-grey hair, wearing a well-tailored suit.

"Gerard?"

"Of course, of course...who else? Mr Gurney...let the gentleman pass."

The bouncer stood reluctantly aside, snarling onion-favoured breath into his face as he passed.

"Come up...let me see you...it's been a long time."

"Ten years."

"Is it really? How time flies!"

After climbing the steps he was led into a spacious office, which must have been above the foyer, with a window that commanded an excellent view over the river. The carpet was thick, the chairs leather, the desk oak—altogether too good, too expensive for such a second-rate night-spot. And the same applied to Anthony himself—immaculate appearance with manners and accent to match.

"What brings you here...old boy?"

"Nancy...and Alison."

Anthony's face dropped.

"Oh...how tedious. I've had just about every muck-raking hack in Christendom trying to bluff their way into here since the child...disappeared. I've told the police everything I know. What, possibly, can I tell you?"

"Alison. Did *you* know she was...*is*...my child?"

Anthony was clearly taken-aback:

"What? My dear boy...I had no idea? I mean...I knew you and her were...how shall I say?...friendly at one time. But if that is so, where have you been for the last ten years?"

"Never mind. Look...did Alison ever accompany Nancy to the club here?"

"Good heavens, no! What are you implying?"

"So what does she do with her when she works here?"

"I really have no idea...and, frankly, I don't care, my dear boy. I'm naturally as distressed as anyone about the child but life goes on and I have a business to run."

Christopher glared at him with contempt:

"Yeah...as always! A business to run!"

"Christopher...are you trying to make some sort of a point?"

"Ollershaw...Harold Ollershaw...know him?"

Anthony noticeably winced but, to his credit, reconstructed the cool persona with admirable efficiency:

"Ollershaw? What do you want with him?"

"So you know him?"

"Harold...Mr Ollershaw has, indeed, from time-to-time, done some art work for us. He's a photographer, as you probably know. He produced those stills outside the club and in the foyer. I believe he has a studio in Tapshed, a few miles from here, on the Exmouth road."

"I know where Tapshed is!"

"My dear boy, calm down. Have a drink. Let's talk about the old days."

"Gerard! I know Harold Ollershaw. I know where his studio is. I was there yesterday. It had been broken into and ransacked. He's disappeared. Any idea where he is?"

Anthony was now eyeing him suspiciously and said, stiffly:

"I'm afraid I have no idea whatsoever. Now, old boy, if it's all the same to you, I have things to do. I should have liked this reunion to have been a little more... convivial...but you seem hell-bent on giving me the third-degree."

He crossed to the door whilst speaking and opened it. At that moment a door across the corridor opened and Christopher found himself looking into a room with a one-way mirror, similar to the one where Nancy/Alison had stood in the video. A dark-haired woman dressed in a schoolgirl uniform, complete with hockey stick, appeared in the doorway and walked off down the corridor. Christopher watched her departing figure—the classic schoolgirl cliché—white blouse, short skirt, knee-length white socks, hat set at a jaunty angle, hair in bunches.

"Still catering for special tastes, I see?"

Anthony frowned:

"Indeed, old boy, but well over the age of consent...if that's what you've been attempting to infer."

Christopher flickered a smile, held Anthony's gaze until he looked away, then headed downstairs.

"Mr Gurney," the voice followed him, "see the gentleman off the premises, if you please."

"Zurtainly. This way zur."

He opened the door and extended his left arm towards Christopher, leaving him in no doubt as to the route he was to take. A strong smell of onions, then a gentle shove helped him on his way.

49
❖ ❖

He had returned home and was sitting in bed with a large glass of chenin blanc, when it occurred to him that he had taken terrible risks that night. Being a detective really didn't suit him. He didn't have a devious, cunning or logical enough mind, capable of calculating in advance the likely outcome of a chain of events. This put him at a serious disadvantage which might even have posed a threat to his life. What did he suppose he was doing at the club? What had he really hoped to achieve? Okay, he had found out that it was definitely the venue for the video but at what cost? For all he knew, Gerard may have had him followed. And how stupid to have mentioned Harry! After all, it may have been Gerard and his henchmen who had 'done over' the studio. Gurney alone looked capable of all that mess.

He switched off the light, slipped out of bed and peered through the curtains. Satisfied that there was no-one lurking outside in the shadows, he returned to bed but sat in the dark meditating. There were so many questions and maybe Harry didn't have all the answers.

But what of Alison...his daughter? If she *had* been abducted and murdered, as now seemed likely, was there some connection with Gerard? Had he really become involved in a child pornography racket? Or had she just been carried off by some itinerant sex-maniac? The more he thought about it, the more his head spun. The wine didn't help but he drank it just the same and poured himself another glass from the bottle on the floor beside the mattress.

The person that baffled him most was Nancy. She must have known about and, presumably, approved of Alison appearing in the video (if, indeed, it was her) and doing goodness knows what else. What could have induced her to do such a thing? Poverty? Blackmail? Or just sheer lack of moral sense? No...no...she wouldn't, couldn't do that. Surely? To do so would mean keeping information from the police even though it might be instrumental to the return of her daughter. As, of course, was he—until tomorrow night when, depending on what Harry had to say, he would either wash his hands of the affair or spill the beans to Harris. What could he get for withholding information? Harris would not be pleased! But *were* the tapes relevant? Supposing the person who had murdered Alison also wrecked Harry's studio looking for the tapes? Wouldn't that point to Gerard? Or, maybe, someone else. The someone with 'special tastes' for whom Harry was holding the tapes. Someone with a lot of money and, perhaps, influence. Someone famous or powerful or both. Someone who could not afford to become involved in a scandal and had panicked when it became apparent that Alison may be dead. Someone who would stop at nothing to cover his tracks. In which case, it was no surprise that Harry had beaten a hasty retreat. Or had he? Maybe he too had been abducted.

Christopher put his head in his hands. It was all completely beyond him and unforgivable that Harry had used him like this.

After the next glass he felt a little more relaxed, slid down the mattress and laid his head on the pillow. For the first time in several days, his finger ached and he

156

remembered that he hadn't taken any of the painkillers that the hospital had prescribed. They were in his pocket downstairs and it seemed too much trouble to fetch them. Closing his eyes, he drifted off into a fitful sleep.

50

❀❀

He sits on the stone altar of a ruined church. A camera approaches and a man asks Him questions. He answers as best he can, speaking fluently but remembering neither questions nor answers. Eventually the interviewer smiles and the camera retreats:

"Thank-you," he says, "I admire your work."

He cringes and looks away, embarrassed by the condescension in the interviewer's voice. It is part of his job to scatter compliments automatically, sometimes recklessly because he wants to be loved by his public and views the interviewee as little more than a springboard for his own ideas and talents. After all, it is *he* who is the real star, the one they all switch on to see, the one who gives his name to the programme itself.

"Come and have a drink," he demands.

He follows.

They sit in a corner of a crowded public house. Everyone recognises him and they nudge each other, wondering why he is talking to someone who they do not recognise. He thrives on being the object of desire and is delighted to interrupt his conversation to sign autographs:

"You know, that short story of yours was very good indeed."

Once again the condescending tone and manufactured smile.

"Short story?"

The smile fades then recovers:

"Yes. The one about the young girl and the apple tree."

"But you are mistaken. I did not write that."

The smile broadens then transforms into a snarl; he leans forward, lips parting, sunlight glinting on a gold tooth:

"Oh but you will, Mr. Purbright, you will."

Outside, there is a stream where the street used to be. All the tarmacadam has been washed away. Children in wellington boots splash around. As He approaches, they turn and run to their mothers. There are railings at the top of the hill against which old men lean and spit into the water. Above their heads, on a curved post, a wind chime tinkles and somewhere someone is burning incense. Two fast flowing streams converge at the bottom of the hill.

He returns to the ruined church and there finds a beautiful young girl. Blond, blue-eyed, dressed only in a long, see-through, nylon veil. As she approaches, He sees the look of admiration and desire in her eyes:

"You must be very famous," her voice soft as the veil, "I saw him interviewing you."

He says nothing. She moves closer. The veil slips to the ground. She trembles as His hands touch her under-developed body. His heart pounds and as His arms close around her, He feels her breath, harsh and irregular, on His neck. He closes His eyes momentarily and she is gone, as if absorbed into His body and He is left standing... naked. Looking down, He sees the veil and wraps it around Himself.

Christopher woke. It was still dark. He turned over, pulled the spare pillow down under the covers and held it tightly against his body...

He is walking along a country lane, feeling good and free, the warm midday sun beating down upon him. But a shadow, as if a cloud, darkens His path and He hears the cries of seagulls. Looking up He sees that they fill the sky: how is it that they do not fly into each other? And there is something else up there, something much bigger. The gulls panic and disperse, the sun shines again but the huge eagle remains hovering above Him. It drops—oh God—the talons bite into his back. He swings around and hits out, knocking it into a ditch at the wayside. But it is unhurt and glares angrily at Him. He walks swiftly away but in an instant it is at his side, keeping pace with Him:

"What is your favourite colour?" it asks, courteously, in an almost human voice.

"Purple," He answers.

"Purple...And what are your interests? And who do you love? And what do you think about...?"

The questions flow. The answers pour from Him as if He is relieved to unburden himself to this stranger. Yet with each answer, He feels correspondingly weakened and the eagle, it seems, noticeably stronger, growing less like a bird and more like a man. The interrogation continues until His mind becomes a blank and He is left standing in the lane, watching helplessly as it walks away in *His* body. A sudden gust of wind ruffles His feathers.

Again, Christopher awoke. It was getting light—the dawn chorus had begun. He turned over with his back to the pillow...

...and found that he was about to enter the courtroom, accused of murder. The chief 'witness' for the prosecution is the victim's overcoat which is said to be possessed of supernatural powers. When confronted by the murderer, these powers will be activated and the coat, assuming a 'life' of its own, will fly at the assailant and attempt to

160

suffocate him by wrapping itself around his head.

He stands in the witness box. The coat is brought in and immediately tears itself from its bearer, swoops across the courtroom and wraps itself around His head. He screams and tears at the material but it tightens around him...

He awoke once more, clutching the pillow to his face, covered in perspiration, heart pounding and fighting for breath. It was nine o'clock. He climbed wearily out of bed, into the bathroom and under the shower.

After breakfast, he recalled a fourth dream which he hastily recorded in a notebook, thinking it a suitably enigmatic ending for his novel. If, indeed, it was ever written...

51

❀ ❀

Spots of rain stung against his face as he walked the deserted Strand in the direction of Goat Walk, a bag tucked under his arm. He turned-up the collar of his coat, hunching and tensing himself against the cold wind blowing down the estuary.

The tide was out—a vast expanse of shingle and mud stretched away into the darkness. Way down on the east side of the estuary he could make out the lights of Exmouth and, much nearer, those of the Royal Marines training camp at Lympstone. Across the river, to the west, it was pitch dark except for the vague outline of the main coastal road to Dawlish, Teignmouth and beyond, highlighted regularly by car headlights—tiny moving spots at that distance—appearing and disappearing behind hedgerows and embankments.

He leaned himself against the lamp post at the end of the Strand and waited. His heart leapt nervously as he heard the church clock commence striking midnight. A bedroom light in the house behind him went out. He grinned to himself, thinking he must look like a character from a Raymond Chandler novel. He glanced along the Goat Walk and then back along the Strand. No sign of anyone. Damn and blast! It was too cold to be playing this kind of game. He glanced at his watch and decided to stay for another five minutes, when he heard the sound of a motor car moving slowly toward him over the shingle below the footpath. Peering into the darkness, he could just make out the shape of a car as it appeared slowly around the corner with its headlights doused. Still some hundred yards away, its engine abruptly cut out; the headlights flashed on and off twice. He looked down at his feet, smiled and shook his head in disbelief. This was ridiculous! Was he seriously expected to walk all that way across mud and shingle? What a bloody nerve! He could damn well come and fetch it himself! He stood his ground. The headlights flashed again. He stood firm but beckoned to the driver. The car started its engine and moved slowly toward him. About fifty yards away it stopped again and flashed its headlights as before. The rain began to fall in earnest. He peered into the gloom but was unable to make-out even the outline of anyone inside the car. Cursing, he walked forward, feet unsteady on the slippery stones. Raindrops on the windscreen made it impossible to identify anyone. When he was within ten yards of the car, the headlights were turned on again, full-beam. Totally blinded, he whirled around cursing and dropping the bag as his arms went instinctively upwards to cover his eyes. Behind him he heard the sound of footsteps on the shingle as someone approached, picked up the bag and retreated to the car. The door was slammed, the car reversed away from him and was gone before he could say a word.

He just stood there, alone, in the darkness, listening to the water trickling through the mud and the occasional eerie bird call from the marshes across the river. Turning and hunching himself against the driving rain, he cursed and headed home.

52

❀ ❀

Without realising—so lost was he in his thoughts—he passed his flat on the Strand and found himself standing outside the house in Mamouth Street. The front door was ajar; he pushed it and stepped inside. The living room door, to his left, was open. Finding no-one, he walked through to the kitchen and conservatory. The french doors were also open; a security light illuminated the garden. Already the lawn needed cutting.

Images of his childhood, spent in that garden, flashed through his mind. His parents had kept chickens at the far end when he was very young and there were apple trees and a vegetable plot as well as a large greenhouse and flower garden. Just outside the back door, where the conservatory now stood, there had been a concrete yard and two out-houses. One was used for storing coal and the other, the larger of the two, which had in his grandmother's day been a wash-house, was a store for useful junk. It was there that he had kept the red pedal car that he drove up and down the garden, shooting Red Indians and assorted wrong-doers en route with his silver six-shooters. The garden had not only doubled for the Wild West but also, as he grew older, Lord's Cricket Ground or Wembley Stadium or St. James' Park, Exeter. Occasionally an ill-directed shot at goal would smash a greenhouse window and often a lofted drive would end-up in a neighbour's flower bed—'six and out'. Some years the garden had been the venue of outdoor birthday parties. He had photographs somewhere of all his schoolfriends seated at a long table on the yard, consuming platefuls of home-made cakes and drinking fizzy lemonade.

The house and garden had changed almost beyond recognition in his time, mostly at the hands of his father, a diligent do-it-yourselfer, but the people and the events still clung to it somehow. Three generations of happiness, despair, struggle, hardship, achievement, defeat, love, life and death.

Retracing his steps, he returned to the kitchen, opening the sliding door to the dining room. There was no-one. Back in the hall, he placed a foot on the stairs, holding the rail set into the wall. Slowly he climbed. At the top, the bathroom and bedroom to his right were both empty as was the master bedroom to his left. The winding attic stairway loomed in front of him. At the top, another open door led into a long raftered room that ran the full length of the house. He felt for the light switch but it didn't work so he stood, listening to the rain pattering on the roof and gusting against the dormer window, trying to accustom his eyes to the gloom. Again he was transported momentarily back to his youth. This had been the room which he had painted black and adorned with mystical symbols and charms. The room in which he had often lain in bed at night and listened, as indeed he did now, to the elements until they lulled him off to sleep. About to turn and go, he noticed something moving at the far end of the room. He stood rooted to the spot, hardly daring to breathe.

53

❀ ❀

"Hello, Christopher..." the voice, coming from out of the gloom, startled him, "...I've been expecting you."

A table lamp with a heavy shade was switched on.

"Come over here where I can see you."

"Oh God...you startled me...look...I'm sorry...the door was open..."

Christopher moved into the room, toward a man seated in a chair by the far wall, in front of a window that overlooked the roofs of the houses in Mamouth Avenue.

"Quite understand...this is your house, after all. Sit here...by the light. Yes...yes...you're just as I imagined."

Christopher nervously took the seat opposite him and found himself looking into the eyes of the very same man who had accompanied Alison to Denby's on Friday night and stared at him as he left with Nancy—the man he had also met, briefly, outside the 'Riverwalk' yesterday. Unable to avert his gaze, Christopher felt those eyes boring right through him, leaving even his innermost thoughts nowhere to hide.

"I'm Mark," he said, and as he said it Christopher experienced a very strong feeling of *deja-vu*, as if he had sat in this very room and had this conversation before.

"How do you do," he spluttered.

Mark burst out laughing:

"Do? Do! That's just it...I can *do* nothing...nothing. Just like you...just like everyone...but tonight will change all that. I'm moving up, you see...moving on."

"Oh...and what's that got to do with me...you said you were expecting me...how can that be?"

"You were here last night...weren't you? But I wasn't ready."

"Yes...I was here...but what is this all about?"

"Christopher...*I'm moving on* [he emphasised these words]...but I can't do that until I have someone to take my place. You are that person, Christopher...*you*. Now listen..." he held up his hand to stop the question that was about to be asked, "I have brought you here for that very purpose and you will have to do the same, one day, if you wish to follow. Do you wish to follow, Christopher?"

He felt his head nodding.

"Good...good. The trouble is that at the moment you're little more than, say, a character in a novel being manipulated by the author. Oh, you think you can *do* things ...you think you can make decisions and shape your own destiny but this is a delusion. *You* can do nothing ...everything is done *to* you."

"I...I don't understand."

"You *must* follow..."

"Why?"

"In order to *do*."

"Yes...I see that...but how?"

He beckoned:

"Have some tea...it's Vintage Darjeeling—leaf, not teabag."

A tray with two teacups and a teapot lay on a low table to his right.

"You don't like tea...but you will like this."

He poured out two cups and dropped in slices of lemon. Christopher grimaced as he was handed the brew.

"Drink and I will answer your question."

Despite himself, Christopher raised the cup to his lips, sipping tentatively at first then, without thinking, draining the rest in two gulps. Returning the cup, he sat back in the chair and relaxed—a satisfying glow spreading throughout his body.

"Good...good. You asked how you were to follow... well...through *mystical experiences*. Remember Dartmoor ... standing above Lustleigh Cleave?"

"How do you know about that?"

"I know everything about you, Christopher...everything. You *must* encourage these experiences."

"But how? They seem so arbitrary and then...so fleeting!"

"The secret is..." he moved closer, beckoning to Christopher, wishing to confide a great secret—a secret for his ears only, "...*attention*. Learn to attend and everything will fall into place. Take this..." he handed Christopher a book. The cover read *First Novel: a novel by Mark Lethbridge-Wright*.

"Is this by you?" unbelievingly.

Mark nodded.

"But I've written a novel with the same title!"

"I know," he smiled, "You must go home now...to Nottingham...and write your next novel. Write it *in order to return*. Then meet me here again."

"But...but I can't just leave now...there's so much to clear up here..."

"Leave that to me. There will be a satisfactory ending, I assure you."

"But...Alison...my daughter..."

He laughed:

"Do you *really* feel anything for her? Is she *really* yours? Or is she just another character in just another novel?"

Christopher fell silent and looked at the floor. He could feel the eyes impelling him to meet their gaze.

"Go home, Christopher, and *write this novel*. Do it."

Without further questioning, Christopher stood, turned and descended the stairs. Flexing his injured hand and feeling neither pain nor stiffness, he took off the strapping around his fingers, bending them with ease. Standing outside on the pavement, he gripped the handle and closed the door on his childhood home.

Appendix 1

❀ ❀

Western Evening Express and Echo
April 21. Late edition.

ALISON—ALIVE AND WELL!

Alison Moltby, the Tapshed schoolgirl missing for two weeks was discovered today alive and well at Birmingham New Street station. Her uncle, Thomas Moltby of Nottingham, has been charged with her abduction. Alison's mother, Nancy, was flown immediately to Birmingham to be re-united with her daughter who was feared dead after being missing for so long. A police statement, released this afternoon, revealed that Alison's uncle, something of a religious fanatic, disapproved of his sister's lifestyle (Nancy was formerly an exotic dancer at the 'Riverwalk' club) and convinced she was not fit to raise a young girl, picked Alison up from school and drove her straight to his house in Nottingham, where she stayed the night. The following morning he took her to a woman friend in Birmingham who kept her locked up for the duration. Alison had gone with her uncle willingly and had believed him when he told her that her mother would be joining them shortly. Detective Superintendent Harris, assigned to the case, commented that he had naturally spoken to Moltby soon after Alison's disappearance but had found no reason to suspect him of having abducted her.

After being locked in a room for several days, the girl eventually escaped through a bathroom window and was found on the concourse of Birmingham New Street station where she had tried to purchase a ticket to Exeter without sufficient money. The teller informed station security and, when it was discovered who she was, the police were brought in.

This brings to an end a massive police hunt for Alison coordinated from the incident room set up at the Matthew's Hall, Tapshed and headed by Detective Superintendent Harris.

Appendix 2

✿ ✿

Western Evening Express and Echo
May 1.

DEVON MAN MISSING

Mark Lethbridge-Wright (pictured below) has been missing from his home in Mamouth Street, Tapshed for ten days. He was last seen by his wife Helen, on Saturday 17th April when she returned to London on a business matter, leaving him alone at their home. Mr Lethbridge-Wright, a poet, was well-known in Tapshed and his wife, a publishing executive for Jonathan Crape, is appealing to anyone who may have seen him after the above date to come forward and contact Devon and Cornwall police.

✿ ✿

Appendix 3

Western Evening Express and Echo
June 3.

TAPSHED MAN'S DEATH AN ACCIDENT

An inquest on the death of Tapshed photographer Harold
Ollershaw whose body was found floating in the Exe off
Lympstone in April, revealed yesterday that he had been
unconscious when he had entered the water and drowned,
having sustained injuries which suggested nothing more
than a heavy fall. Mr Ollershaw had owned a boat on the
Exe, moored at Tapshed, and traces of his blood were
found in a dingy tied to the boat which was still at its
mooring. Two suitcases were also found in the dingy
suggesting that Mr Ollershaw was planning a vacation
when he seemingly slipped and fell into the water striking
his head.

A verdict of accidental death was recorded.

❈ ❈

Now Available:
I.S.B.N. 0-946650-71-3. £6.95.

First Novel

a novel by

Colin Stanley

"Do what you will, this Life's a fiction
And is made up of Contradiction."

❀ ❀ ❀

These lines from William Blake do little to prepare the reader for
the extraordinary events that unfold in this unconventional thriller
where fact and fiction merge unnervingly.
The action, switching between Tapshed, a small town in Devon, and
London, focuses upon the police hunt for a missing schoolgirl.
The hero, a minor but published poet, in the process of writing his
first novel, unwittingly drawn into a dark underworld of pornography and paedophilia, becomes a suspect.
But nothing is as it seems and the chance discovery of a missing
chapter from the novel confirms Blake's view of the state of things.

❀ ❀ ❀

"A splendid metaphor...a rare and intelligent novel by a rare and
intelligent novelist..."

Mark Lethbridge-Wright
Sunday Chronicle

Paufict presents:

Laura Del Rivo's first novel since
Daffodil on the Pavement (1967)

SPEEDY
AND
QUEEN KONG

A Novel by
Laura Del Rivo

"Speedy was poor but dishonest. He could not read or write well, but he could count...Half his mind was robot, clickety-click, cool as an ice-cube, cool to the point of total refrigerated insensibility...The other part was sensationalist. He exploded braincells that irradiated the loft under his skull with electric blue lightwaves."

"Queen Kong had dyed orange hair, erect in a crest. She went in for tight T-shirts. Most T-shirts were tight on Queen Kong; she was a weighty lady who led with the chest...She dyed her hair orange to blaze out her last passion; for she was getting on in weight and years; for Speedy."

Just two of the larger-than-life characters from this extraordinary novel by the author of *The Furnished Room* (filmed by Michael Winner as *West 11*).

❀ ❀ ❀

"A virtuoso performance...a poetic phantasmagoria...Del Rivo shows her mastery of a stabby aphoristic style, impaling her characters on the tips of vicious metaphors...The narrative crackles with jokes and apt observations...(one is reminded of Joe Orton who savours and celebrates the spiritual impoverishment of his characters)." **Paul Newman**, Editor of *Abraxas* and author of *Murder as an Antidote for Boredom: the novels of Laura Del Rivo, Colin Wilson and Bill Hopkins*.

"She writes brilliantly...this book achieves its effects by means of satirical caricature, rather like Nathanael West's masterpiece *Miss Lonelyhearts*..." **Colin Wilson** (from his *Afterword*).

❀ ❀ ❀

ISBN:0-946650-85-3
Paper. 111pp. £7.95. November 2004.
www.pauperspress.com
e-mail: books@pauperspress.com

Paufict
And the makers of 'Nasty Nibbles',
the soggy unsavoury snacks that actually putrefy in
your mouth
present:

Colin Stanley's
Sense-less book of complete
nonsense.

**Illustrated by Maggie Guillon
and Yvonne Harrison**

Ever wondered about the formation of the asteroids,
the mating habits of *Frudes*, or why the *Chronically
A-Symmetric Grouse* seldom entertains?
Ever considered philosophy as an alternative form of
entertainment?
Want to know why Sir Barty Dingwell-Bore haunts the
churchyard from five past twelve 'til four?

*Well...put your feet in a bucket of cream and
Read this book!*

"Nothing to grouse about" – Colonel Bagshot Humming-Brooke.
"Mortifyingly good" – the late H. Lampton Frizbee-Bell.

ISBN 0-946650-84-5
Available: Jan 2004.Price £5.95.68pp.
www.pauperspress.com